The author and translator, Kokilam Subbiah, was once actively involved in the unionising of Tamil labourers, especially women, in the Sri Lankan tea plantations. She has taught Tamil and Dravidian linguistics at the University of Chicago and has a Master of Fine Arts degree from the Art Institute of Chicago, and has held one-woman shows in India. She now lives in Texas.

AF622295

MIRAGE

KOKILAM SUBBIAH

Translated from the Tamil
Thoorathu Pachai
by
KOKILAM SUBBIAH

Orient BlackSwan

ORIENT BLACKSWAN PRIVATE LIMITED

Registered Office
3-6-752, Himyatnagar, Hyderabad 500 029 (A.P), India
Email: centraloffice@orientblackswan.com

Other Offices
Bangalore, Bhopal, Bhubaneshwar, Chennai
Ernakulam, Guwahati, Hyderabad, Jaipur, Kolkata
Lucknow, Mumbai, New Delhi, Patna

© Orient Blackswan Private Limited
First Published by Orient Longman Private Limited 2006
First Orient Blackswan Impression 2009

© Series and cover design
Orient Blackswan Private Limited

The Tamil original of Mirage *(Thoorathu Pachai)*
was first published in 1964 by Tamil Puthakalayam, Chennai.

ISBN 13: 978-81-250-3070-6

Typeset by
Universal Print Systems Limited
Chennai 600 008

Printed in India at
Novena Offset
Chennai 600 005

Published by
Orient Blackswan Private Limited
160, Annasalai, Chennai 600 002
Email: chennai@orientblackswan.com

This book is dedicated

to

my friend and mentor
Kamil Zvelebil

and

all the women working

in the tea plantations of Sri Lanka

Contents

Preface

Thoorathu Pachai, the Tamil original of *Mirage* was published in the year 1964—it has taken another forty years for me to recreate this book in English. This book is an attempt to bring to the fore the unchronicled, unvoiced lives of the indentured labourers from India working on the tea plantations of Sri Lanka—in that sense it is social history in the form of fiction.

As a convent-educated daughter of a civil servant in Sri Lanka, I knew nothing about life in the tea plantations. But marriage (my husband was the Member of Parliament representing the plantation workers) brought me in direct contact with their tragic lives. I gradually became deeply interested in their work and welfare. I organised a women's movement and in a bid to bring global attention to their plight, I took two of these workers to speak at an international women's conference in Germany.

At Prague, Czechslovakia, I met Dr. Kamil Zvelebil, a renowned Indologist, sitting at a dusty desk and poring over a Tamil lexicon. During the communist regime he was not allowed to go to India; he was so thrilled to meet me because I was a Tamil. I sent him books and translations on my return to India and thereby a friendship developed, that has lasted over fifty years. I told him about my work on the plantations and about the women workers. He said I must write their story, whatever it takes.

I did not believe I was a writer, though I had written articles for newspapers. I did not have the confidence to write their story, which was not an easy one to begin with. But on Mr. Zvelebil's insistence I eventually undertook the task. I spoke to these workers, old and young, traveled extensively and sought to understand their life and history. My interaction also brought me in touch with the kanganys (supervisors) and the white superintendents who had enormous power over their lives. Most of the incidents narrated in this book are culled from real-life stories and are not figments of the imagination.

This book is a homage to the stoic lives of thousands of indentured labourers who gave their lives to these plantations. I dedicate this book to my friend and mentor, Dr. Zvelebil, without whose encouragement this book would not have been written. It was also he who gave me the name of the publisher I should go to—Tamil Puthakalayam. The owner and editor Sri Kn Muthiah took one look at it and decided to publish it. This was in 1964. I would also like to thank Sri Chidambara Raghunathan, writer and novelist, for his editorial support to *Thoorathu Pachai.*

The world needs to hear the story of these hard-working, exploited, uncared-for people—and hence the novel.

Kokilam Subbiah
June 2006

1

It was a very small village. Even today, in the year 1964, you will only see a single winding track leading to it. There were no wide roads to speak of, and who knows how many more centuries it would take for a proper one to be laid?

Three miles away from the village you do come across a rudimentary road, laid with red earth by the government, to facilitate motor transport. The people from the village will have to reach this road to make their purchases from one of the five shops that have cropped up by the bus stop.

If this is the situation today, you can imagine how the village must have been a hundred years ago.

In those days, there were only about forty or fifty families living in this village called Senthur. And among these, only seven or eight lived within its precincts, isolated from the rest who were housed in the cheri, in the outskirts of the village.

There would not have been more than three hundred people in this village. In addition, there were four or five dogs, ten or twelve cats, thirty to forty goats, seven or eight buffaloes and a few cows.

Among those who lived within the village were a temple priest, the landlord Jambulingam Pillai, his son-in-law, the school teacher Kalyanaraman, besides two Chettiars who dealt with money-lending.

In the cheri there were a few who owned one or two acres of land. But most of them were landless labourers who paid rent to the mirasdar. In short, it could be said that the people living in the cheri worked on the lands of the Mirasdar who owned most of the village. Velan's family was one among them.

The mirasdar of Senthur was Sethulingam Pillai. He owned most of the wet and dry lands of village, but he did not live in Senthur. The mirasdar lived about ten miles away from Senthur, in a village called Mavalur, in a charming three-storeyed house, with his three wives.

The mirasdar hardly knew anything about Senthur. Once in a while, if he happened to go past the village, he probably looked around with mild interest. The harvesting of the fields and the safe passage of the harvested grains to the mirasdar's granary, were all taken care of by his kanakapillai and clerk. His kanakapillai, Vyapuri, and clerk, Veerapandian, carefully attended to all his needs and kept him happy.

Velan owned about half an acre of land and a hut. There was a majestic neem tree in the yard in front of his hut. Even though it belonged to Velan, it was a common congregating area for the people of the cheri. It was under this neem tree that all the people gathered in the evenings. They swept it clean and made the place pleasant by smearing it with cow dung. There was a string cot under the tree and Velan slept on it. When he was not sleeping on it, the people of the cheri sat on it, gossiped, spinned yarns, told stories, settled disputes, and talked about the good and bad happenings in the village.

One day, Velan sat on his cot, deep in thought, as he shoved betel leaves into his mouth. He chewed betel all day long much like cattle chewing cud. Life was unthinkable without betel-chewing for Velan.

The time was just right for an afternoon nap. Not that Velan, a farm hand, could afford to indulge in one. Besides, the uncomfortable emptiness in his stomach was not conducive for sleep.

Unable to set his mind at rest, Velan rose hurriedly from the cot, gathered his long hair and tried to tie it into a knot. His matted, unkempt hair resisted the attempt a few times. He shook a piece of cloth, now encrusted with dust and stains of the red soil, and casually flung it over his shoulders and started walking. He would not have gone a few yards when he felt someone following him. Turning around he saw that it was his daughter Valli.

'Valli, why are you out in this heat? Go home,' he ordered.

'No Appu, I want to come with you,' said Valli, as she tightly caught hold of her father's vetti and held on to him.

'Listen to me when I say no. I am on my way to Saruhani. I cannot take you with me. If you walk all the way in this heat, you will faint. Go, go to your mother!'

Valli did not listen, she kept following him.

'I said go home. You have had no food. You might get dizzy and faint. Go,' admonished Velan.

She continued walking behind her father and soon the heat got to her. She stopped to rest under a tamarind tree, her father kept walking without looking back.

Valli gazed up the tamarind tree and was delighted to find a few fruits on the upper branches. She was only seven or eight years old and knew that she would not reach them. She contented herself by chewing on a few tender leaves that were within her reach.

Hunger pangs and the scorching heat lulled her senses. A gentle breeze blew across the landscape. The child fell asleep under the tree.

Valli wore nothing more than a tattered skirt. The skirt looked like it had not been washed for weeks. The skirt was so ragged that it would be pointless to count the number of holes in it. She was not even old enough to be able to tie the skirt properly on her waist and most often than not, she just held on to it.

But there was a certain charm to Valli's dark face. This shone through her dirt-encrusted, matted hair and the lean, under-nourished body. Her hair stank of neem oil and was infested with lice. But she slept peacefully under the tree.

A few goats and cattle were grazing in the adjoining fields. There was no green grass to be had due to the drought. The animals grazed around hoping at least to find some straw.

Senthur and the villages surrounding it had been affected by drought and famine. And this has been the condition for the past three years.

In Ramnathapuram district, lack of rains for even a year could cause a famine. Can you imagine the plight of the people when they have had no rains for the past three years? The pond in the village had dried up a long time ago. The fish in the pond were also long gone. As if that was not enough, even the well from which they got their drinking water was completely dry.

'Maybe it is Time avenging the wickedness on earth? Or a terrible curse cast on the village?' The villagers wondered among themselves, quite despondently. The fields that had been filled with golden-eared paddy, were now parched and cracked. The stubble from the previous harvest now stood out like spiked thorns piercing the soles of their feet, making them bleed. But then, most of them had little blood in their bodies, thanks to the famine. The goats and cattle had pulled out even the roots in their quest for food. Now they had nothing to graze on. Heat and hunger, took its toll and many fell dead along the fields.

Who could endure a drought for over three years? Hunger and starvation preyed upon the village. Many just perished in the heat. Instead of the golden-eared grain swaying in the wind, there were only the skeletons of dead animals, left by the feasting vultures.

Velan was one of those struggling inhabitants of Senthur. Velan's family was large—he had two wives and nine children. Before the onset of drought he had had four goats, two bullocks for ploughing the field and a buffalo that gave them milk. That was before the famine. Now he owned no animal. The half acre of land that he owned, had been mortgaged to the mirasdar two years ago. Velan was unable to pay the interest or the tax for it. There had been no farm work for the past three years. Nine children and two wives were all that he had. There was nothing else that belonged to him.

Velan's first wife was Sellatha. Once, when he had gone to his uncle's house, he had seen Sellatha working in the field. He fell in love and married her. But his grandmother insisted that he should marry his aunt's daughter, Muthamma. Respecting her wishes he married Muthamma, and brought her home as his second wife. It was more than twelve years since he married Sellatha, and ten years since he wed Muthamma.

There was not much in common between Sellatha and Muthamma. Sellatha had a big mouth and was quarrelsome. Can you imagine her providing a docile welcome to Muthamma? Sellatha was malicious, and never let her live in peace. In fact, Velan too feared her tongue. Sellatha was jealous of the fact that Muthamma was better looking than her. Amidst such circumstances Sellatha had six children and Muthamma had four. Sellatha's last child had died almost a year ago.

The quiet and naive Muthamma suffered much from the loud-mouthed Sellatha.

Unable to put up with their daily skirmishes, the people in the cheri ordered Velan to build a separate dwelling for Muthamma. So Muthamma's hut was built next to Sellatha's and they even shared a wall. Velan's income was to be divided between the two families. As a result, Muthamma found it difficult to even partially satisfy the hunger of her family.

Muthamma had four children—the eldest was Suppan, second came Rengan, third was Valli, and the fourth was a baby called Papathi.

Velan struggled to meet the demands of the two families.

2

Valli, sleeping on the thinnai, woke up with a start on hearing the beating of the thandora. Her brothers Rengan and Suppan ran outside.

'Valli! Valli! Come let us go and see what's happening!' Rengan shouted as he ran with Suppan. Valli holding her skirt in one hand, ran after them.

'Listen everyone! Listen! Men are needed to go to Kandy land. All those who wish to go, go see Karuppiah Kangany. Go see him immediately. You will be paid well! You will be paid well! Go see him immediately!' The man shouted as he beat the drum.

All the people of the cheri crowded around to watch the fun.

'Instead of dying here of starvation it is better that we go and die there,' said a few.

'Chi! Who wants to go die in an unknown land? Even if we die, let us die here, in our own land. Why go there?' said some. Different opinions were expressed.

'If we believe all that they say, we will be cheated. The grass always appears greener on the other shore.'

'Yes, who knows how it will be there? Aren't they all of the same caste? Do you think we will survive if we listen to them?' some said in frustration.

'Of those who had gone earlier, only a few have returned and they have nothing good to say. We are compelled to believe what the kangany has to say.'

'Valli, what are you doing here? Renga, take her home, it is getting dark,' said Velan.

'Sella! I too have decided to go to Kandy,' Velan told Sellan, who was his neighbour.

'Why Vela? What will we do if you leave?' asked a shocked Sellan.

'What can I do about that? If we stay here any longer, we will die of starvation. Valli, tie your skirt properly before you go child.'

'Ayya, are we also leaving the village?' asked Valli, holding on to her father's hand.

'Don't listen to elders' talk and go repeating it. Go home now.'

'Ayya, Amma told me that when you come home she will make kanji for us. Have you brought anything for us Appu?' asked Valli with an expectant look.

Velan was pained looking at Valli's piteous face. How much longer will the child's tender body survive starvation, Velan wondered in agony.

'Go home. I will go get some kambarisi from Kathan and come.'

'Really Appu?' asked Valli, her face lighting up.

'Yes, child, I will bring kambarisi,' said Velan. Valli slowly walked back to their hut.

'Annachi, what are you going to do with all that land?' asked Sellan.

'What land? All that was mortgaged two years ago to the mirasdar. Do you think he is going to give it back to us?' asked Velan with a cynical smile.

Velan and Sellan walked home slowly, talking about their uncertain future.

'Suppa, go to Kathan's shop and ask him to give you a measure of kambu and a measure of solam,' Velan called out to his son as he reached his hut.

'Muthamma, Suppan will bring some grain, make some kanji for Valli,' said Velan as he sat under the neem tree.

Sellatha stuck her head out of the adjacent hut.

'What is this? Does this not look like a house to you? Don't we look like human beings? There is no one to ask about us, even if we die of starvation, while that woman eats well and grows fat. You think you can starve us to death?' Sellatha raged at Velan.

'Don't bray like an ass! I have asked for some for you too. What do you know? I am to be blamed for being kind to you! A man slogs and slaves all day in this heat and somehow brings home some money and all he gets is a screaming devil!' He spat at her.

'There she is, that clever scheming bitch!' Sellatha swore, pointing at Muthamma. She dragged her son Ramu and started beating him, 'Saniyan! Crying all the time. Moodevi! What can you do, except starve to death?' She flung the child outside the hut.

Velan unconcerned, called out to Muthamma.

'Ey Muthamma, Karuppiah Kangany said we have to leave next pournami day for Kandy. I have signed over my lands to the mirasdar. We have to reach Kandy somehow with whatever little we get from the deal,' Velan said, folding a betel leaf and shoving it into his mouth.

Velan thought over what he had told Karuppiah Kangany. It was not as if he did not understand that his family circumstances were deteriorating. He had sold all that he possessed long ago for food. He had nothing more to sell now.

Since the drought had set in, there had been no work on the farm. Occasionally there was work for the women in the big farms—husking paddy, cleaning ragi or shelling lentils. Otherwise there was absolutely no work for them. How long could they live with no means of survival?

'Sellatha, come here. I have decided to go to Kandy. Instead of dying here, I think it is better to go to this unseen land. Will you also come with us?' Velan asked.

Sellatha, who was standing outside the hut with hands on her hips, approached the cot on which Velan was seated, fuming with anger.

'What did you say? Go to Kandy? Who wants to go that far? As though we are going to make our fortune in that faraway land! Why should I go so far leaving all our kith and kin? Did you think I am also a destitute like that woman?' she said, referring to Muthamma.

'What kith and kin are you talking about? Are they the ones feeding you? I have decided to go whether you like to come or not. Muthamma, are you coming or are you also staying behind?' asked Velan, his voice neutral, expressing neither enthusiasm nor bitterness.

'Why do we have to go such a long way? Do you think it is possible to drag these children all that far?' Muthamma asked in a faint voice filled with fear.

'You are another one! There are many like us, we are not the only ones going, you know? Anyone who wishes to come with me may come. I am definitely going even if I have to go alone,' Velan said with determination.

'Appu, I am coming with you!' declared Valli running up to him.

'It will be enough if you alone come with me, child. It does not matter if no one else comes,' said Velan hugging her.

'Have you signed the land over to the mirasdar?' asked Sellatha.

'Yes. What do you want me to do? The kanakapillai claims the interest had gone over the cost of the land, so they took it.'

'If that is the case, what do you think we are going to live on?' she demanded.

'What is it to you? You can only talk like a big shot with your big mouth. Just shut up. Don't make me lose my temper! Just go,' Velan said, fuming with anger.

Sellatha suspected Velan must have gotten some money from somewhere and gotten drunk.

'What do you care? You have sold the land and taken taken care of yourself. I am the one who has to suffer here,' she said, boiling with anger and hate.

Velan's control snapped, 'Do I have to ask your permission to buy or sell my property? As if you have brought it from your father's house? She talks as if she's the one who brought it.'

'Yes, that's right, you earned it all by yourself. If I had not slogged so hard what would you have had—a big stink?' she answered defiantly.

'You dare talk back to me? You have become that arrogant have you?' Velan grabbed Sellatha by the hair and pushed her down to the floor and began to thrash her mercilessly. The neighbours had to intervene to separate them.

Sellatha picked up her child and went towards the thinnai, crying.

'Vela, what's going on here?' asked Muthamma's uncle as he walked in. 'Is it true that you are leaving for Kandy?'

'Thatha, we are all going with Appu. Will you also come with us?' said Valli, as she embraced the old man.

'No, my darling child! I have become an old man. I can hardly see. How can I come so far?' he said, as he lifted her up to kiss her.

'We have to go away somewhere, leaving behind this cursed life. What else can we do? I am leaving on the next pournami day,' said Velan tiredly.

'Wherever you go, as long as you and your family are alright, I'll be happy,' said the old man, as he sat on the cot.

'Mama have some kanji before you leave. Muthamma bring some kanji for Mama if you have some ready. Mama, why don't you sleep here tonight and go in the morning? Otherwise you will be stumbling in the dark.' said Velan concerned.

'Chinnayya, have some kanji before you leave. Come wash your hands and drink some kanji,' said Muthamma, as she brought a sembu filled with water.

Velan and the old man went into the hut to have their kanji.

Even though the sun that scorched the land all day had hidden himself now, the wind that was blowing was hot and relentless. The weak rays of the moon filtered through the barren trees.

Valli having drunk her kanji, her long uncared for belly satiated, was now playing outside. Some kanji had spilled on her clothes and was crusted around her mouth. Suddenly, as she was playing, she began to retch.

'Amma! Appa! Valli is vomiting!' shouted Rengan.

Muthamma caught the exhaused Valli just as she was about to fall. 'Having been hungry for such a long time, her stomach couldn't handle the food. Here, wash your mouth child,' she said in a voice filled with pain.

Velan wondered at the truth in Muthamma's statement.

'Sivalingam's cattle died yesterday, including the two oxen, poor fellow,' said the old man.

'Even my brother's cow died. It went to graze in the field, fell down and could not get up. It's stomach had shrunk and it died the same day. Now there's no milk for the baby. They are giving her ragi kanji. They say even that does not agree with the child's stomach. Her mother died of starvation after childbirth. Now my brother has a hard time managing on his own,' said Velan.

'Your brother has had trouble since his wife died. Let that be. What are you going to do with your lands?' asked the old man.

'What can I do? The mirasdar asked me to sign all the land over to him. He said the interest was more than the cost of the land, the crook.' As he said the words, Velan choked with pain and sadness. His kanji tasted bitter, he could not have any more of it.

'Here Renga, finish this. I've had enough,' said Velan rising to wash his hands.

'What a lot of misery people have to suffer in this life,' he thought to himself.

'Let me know the day you will be leaving. I will come to wish you well,' said the old man as he took leave of Velan.

Velan saw Valli in the dim moonlight, curled up in a corner of the thinnai.

'Whatever happens I am definitely going to Ceylon,' he promised himself.

ଔ

Valli, sitting on a branch of the neem tree, watched her mother gathering their things for the journey.

'Atha, are we taking all these little things with us, the torn mats, that winnower?' Valli kept plying Muthamma with endless questions. The children grew excited as the day of their departure drew near.

Velan wondered how he was going to take his two wives and nine children with him. As if she meant to solve his problem, Sellatha refused to go with him. He too thought it best if she did not accompany him.

Sellatha believed that Velan would earn money in Ceylon and send enough home for her and her children.

Velan decided to take only Muthamma and her children with him. Going away from the land one was born in, leaving behind one's kith and kin to make one's living in an alien land, was a frightening prospect. Doubts and misgivings took hold of him as days passed by. Who knew what kind of trials awaited him? Fear squeezed his heart. Outside, the sun blazed forth, inside, his mind was scorched by the fire of fear and uncertainty that burned his body and soul.

3

On that momentous day too, the sun rose in the east. As usual it spread its intense heat on the world, scorching it, as if it was angry with it. It was the day of pournami. Even though the sun had risen as usual in the eastern sky, for some in Senthur village, the sunlight had acquired an added glow. Everything looked and felt new. There was a pervasive love and affection for all things and beings. They looked at everything with new eyes.

Valli, lying on Velan's lap, looked keenly at the tamarind and elandai trees that had already shed their fruits, long before they matured, due to the drought.

'Appu, are there elandai trees in that foreign land?' she asked.

'I am sure there are, my child.'

'Are there any tamarind and neem trees too?

'Yes, there will be those as well.'

'Will we be living in a hut like this?' Valli continued to badger her father with questions.

Velan was engrossed with all kinds of disturbing thoughts. Valli's questions only made him apprehensive and tense.

'Appu, we will come back to our village, won't we?' she asked again.

'Did you think we will be staying there for good? Of course, we will be returning soon,' promised Velan. Was this statement meant to reassure him or Valli?

* * *

He looked at the fields stretching into the distance. At this time of the year, there should have been golden-eared paddy dazzling under the sun. Instead, he only saw the parched, cracked earth spread out before him. The thought choked him with grief. Was this going to be their fate—with no happiness to look forward to, ever? Thinking along these lines he fumed and fretted.

What was the assurance that the new life he was going to step into would be any different? Who knew what kind of difficulties, adversities and failures awaited them? His mind felt like it was caught in a whirlpool.

He knew that he was not going to change his mind. Come what may, he was firm in his decision to go to Ceylon.

'Are we going to carry all these bundles with us?' asked Valli.

'Yes,' murmured Velan.

'Are we going to take these torn mats with us? Can't we get new ones there?'

'We will. But nothing like taking our own mats with us.' Velan answered patiently.

'Does that mean we cannot get mats like these over there?'

'Go! Go and play! Tell Atha that I am going to see Mookan. I will return soon. As soon she brings water, wash your hands and feet,' ordered Velan as he walked away.

☙

His imagination flew to the time when he would return from Ceylon bringing plenty of money—he would build a big house and live in peace and happiness. He dreamt of gold coins lying in wait at the roots of the tea and coffee bushes. He fantasised about coming back to Senthur, with people looking at him with awe and respect. He also dreamt of finding a good groom from a good family for Valli.

In that sweltering heat, no one in the village slept that night. People gathered on the thinnais of their huts. It being a full moon night, all the trees and huts were clearly outlined and visible. The sound of people tying their belongings could be heard everywhere. The noise of their chatter reverberated, disturbing the quiet of the night. The full moon flooded the village making all that it touched gleam brightly. Time and circumstances were waiting to change the lives of these people from the cheri in different ways.

They discussed over and over again the bygone days, and the good and the bad in the life they had enjoyed, till they were really tired and exhausted. The shrill cry of a jackal rent the night air and broke the noisy gossip of the cheri. Midnight had passed and a gullible crow, looking at the full moon, began to caw thinking it was dawn. People who were setting out on this journey gathered their belongings on hearing the crow. They woke the sleeping children. There was excitement and anticipation in the air.

Somewhere a cock crowed and ceased.

'Are you all ready for the journey?' enquired Karuppiah Kangany, announcing his arrival.

'Yes ayya, we are ready.'

In the light of the full moon they could see Karuppiah Kangany standing under the neem tree in full regalia—an umbrella in his hand, a turban on his head, a long coat whose colour was difficult to identify in the dark. He had folded and tied his vetti above his knees, and he wore sandals on his feet. A pair of diamond earstuds twinkled in the moonlight. He had a long moustache that flowed down his face and you could see his long hair tied in a neat bun under his turban. He looked very dandy.

'Vela, get all the people to gather under the neem tree. It will be easier for me to take the count.' The kangany's assistant was standing behind him in a corner, respectful and meek. 'Come here Singaram, count the number of people here. I will go and get the rest of them,' said the kangany as he strode away.

Within a short while, all the people who were making the journey gathered under the neem tree.

They heard the kangany's voice as he returned, 'Is everyone ready?'

'They have been ready for a long time now.'

'Vela, are your children and the rest ready?'

'Yes, ayya.'

'Is this all you have?' the kangany asked, looking at the two bundles that Velan had.

'Yes ayya, we don't have much to take? Besides, you had told us that if we carry too much it will be difficult for us to walk long distances,' said Velan.

'That's right. It is better that you carry as little as possible. Just a few essential things that are necessary for the journey. A few pots and pans, some ragi and kambu, since it will be difficult to get food on the way,' said the Kangany.

He counted all of them like they were heads of cattle.

'Here, will you carry Valli, I will carry the bundle,' said Muthamma. She had a bundle on her head, the baby on her hips, and the mats in her hand. Suppan carried two bundles and Rengan being the small one, carried the waterpot.

Velan carried Valli on his shoulders.

'Papathi, Our Devi! Please protect us.' Each one called out the name of their family deity to be their protector as they started walking. They walked in single file like ants crawling along the fields. In the moonlight, their fields, the village in which they had lived and birthed their children—all of it assumed a new look. Somewhere in the distance they heard the crows cawing.

Far away they saw a faint glimmer of light in the eastern sky. The sun was spreading its rays.

'Appu, Appu! Look there! Look there, can you see the sky all red? What is it? Is it blood that you see there?' Valli asked in wonder, swinging her legs on his shoulders.

'That child, is the sign of dawn,' replied Velan.

In that twilight hour, their shadows looked like tiny dark creatures crawling along the fields. Some of them turned around and looked at their receding village, now just a little speck. They could see nothing else.

In the morning light one saw that all those walking along in rows were mostly young men. Only one or two were married men who had left their wives behind. There were only two men bringing their families—Velan was one among them. In the 1800s when coolies went to Ceylon they did not take their womenfolk and children with them.

It looked like they were on a march.

'Ayya, I am hungry,' Valli whimpered.

'Wait a little longer, as soon as we reach the next village I will make some kanji for you,' Velan tried pacifying her.

As the sun rose higher, the heat grew worse and the children grew tired and limp. Can you imagine what happens when children become exhausted?

There was a lot of murmuring as they saw a building far away in the distance. They saw a few figures moving around.

'We can have kanji as soon as we reach that village,' said Velan.

'We have reached the ambalam, now we can cook, eat and take some rest,' said the kangany with a flourish.

'Ambalam, what is that?' they asked not understanding him.

'We will be resting every ten miles in ambalams that have been built for people who are going to the tea estates,' explained Singaram, the kangany's assistant.

As they came closer, they noticed that like them there were many more people who were going to Ceylon.

'Where are those people from?' asked Valli.

'They are like us, from other villages, going to Kandy,' explained Velan. There was a strange excitement in his voice. Seeing all those people going to Ceylon like them, gave the people of Senthur courage and boosted their enthusiasm, as they believed they had a future waiting for them in Ceylon.

4

The ambalam was a long shed, with a thatched roof of coconut palms. In those days, the rich built sheds like these in every town as rest-houses for poor wayfarers. It had no walls and everywhere you saw people in groups, chatting and cooking. Karuppiah Kangany's people from Senthur found some space for themselves and settled with their belongings. It was an arid, barren place, interspersed with a few tamarind, elandai and neem trees. The summer heat had scorched most of the other trees dry. There were no permanent dwellers living in that area. If not for that ambalam there would not be any signs of human habitation. The travellers from Senthur gathered firewood, fetched water from a well which was almost dry, and started cooking.

'Valli, don't wander too far away. Suppa, take care of her, will you?' called out Muthamma. Velan sat in a corner, immersed in his own thoughts, folding betel leaves and stuffing it in his mouth. Valli came running and plonked herself on his lap.

'When are we going back home, Ayya?' asked Valli.

'We will go, my child. Very soon, we will,' replied Velan absently.

'Come, let's go back home, Appa!' pleaded Valli, yearning for her home.

She was not the only one yearning for home. Even Velan longed for the home and village he had left behind. The sorrow and pain he felt in his heart seared his soul. There was no one to whom he could voice his troubles.

He did not know where his decision to leave his home and village was going to lead him. Selling his lands and porperty, he has left his village with his wife and children—he has embarked on this adventure like a nomad. He wondered if he had made a wise decision.

That he would achieve the happiness he wished for in a faraway country, leaving his misfortunes behind, was not a certainty. Increasingly, these doubts disturbed his thoughts and confused his mind. Unfortunately, a few incidents that took place on the way gave credence to these doubts.

Karuppiah Kangany did not seem like the same man who had recruited them in the village. There was no evidence of the benevolent, considerate kindliness he had exhibited earlier.

'Hey! You, go sit there in the corner!' 'Do this!' 'Do that!' 'You must not sleep here, what is this?' He ordered stridently, throwing his weight around.

'Get up! Go outside!' He nudged and prodded the children with his walking stick. All this scared Velan. The kangany's attitude in the village had been quite different. Then, he had used honeyed words. Now, his speech had turned to something sinister. All those who had left Senthur with him noticed the difference.

'What's this? Kangany ayya's talk seems to have changed,' said one man.

'Don't you know, this is only the beginning. We will soon know what kind of man the kangany really is,' said another.

'What is the use of worrying now. Even if you run miles away, your sins will follow you!'

People were disgusted and disillusioned by the Kangany's attitude.

'All of you have your food and get some rest. We leave for Devipattinam at dusk,' shouted the kangany.

'Come and have some kanji,' called out Muthamma, seated near the fire feeding the baby.

Velan noticed that Valli had fallen asleep on his lap. 'Get up Valli. Have some kanji and then go to sleep,' he said.

Just as dusk crept in, Muthamma bundled all their belongings once again and looked around to see if there were other women. There were a few women scattered among the crowd in the ambalam. Muthamma felt consoled, even though she could not talk to them. The baby began to whimper and cry. She had no milk in her breasts as she herself was starved. What could she do, the poor woman?

Velan, on waking up, found Muthamma seated beside him. He felt an affection for her which he had never felt before. Her abject trust and unfailing belief in him, made his weary face soften with compassion and gentleness. He sat there motionless in thought. He saw tears on her face as she fed the baby. The baby, hoping to draw some milk from her breasts, sucked and dragged, only to find that there was no milk. It began to wail. Velan was determined to somehow make amends and set things right for her and his family.

'Get up! Get up!' shouted Karuppiah Kangany, nudging people with his umbrella.

As they woke up and gathered their bundles, the kangany did a head-count and his assistant checked the list of names to see if all of them were there. They should reach Devipattinam the next evening and by the following evening, Rameswaram, another coastal town. The Kangany kept prodding people to hasten them.

'I wonder why we ever embarked on this journey,' complained Muthamma.

'My legs are paining,' cried Valli feebly.

'You could have also stayed with Sellatha. Did I ask you to come with me?' asked Velan, annoyed with her.

'We should have stayed in our village, even if we had to survive with very little or no food. I don't know what we are doing, dragging these children all that distance,' grumbled Muthamma. Even though Velan knew she was right, he was angered by her words.

By the time they reached Devipattinam, darkness had set in and there was no light anywhere except a small lamp that was lit in the ambalam. The moon had not yet risen, though a few stars twinkled in the sky. They could not see any trees or houses in the faint light.

The ambalam which had been quiet so far, was now noisy with the bustling of the people who had just arrived. The sound of twigs being broken and the lighting of cooking fires compounded the racket.

Velan laid the sleeping Valli in a corner and went out to get some firewood. He did not wish to send the boys into the dark night.

'Atha, I am going to sleep,' said Suppan, as he dropped down exhausted.

'Renga, go see if you can find some water somewhere,' said Muthamma in a tired voice. In the darkness, the shadows looked like giant demons moving around. The Kangany's bullying sounded like the howls of the devil.

As Velan gathered firewood he noticed that there were a few neem and puvarasan trees. After he gave the wood to Muthamma, he tied a cloth cradle on the branch of the puvarasan tree and put the baby to sleep.

Meanwhile the stars had come out. He could see clouds gathering at a distance. Velan stared at the clouds which he noticed came from the direction of their village, which they had left only a few days ago to escape the drought. He had no doubts about it. The clouds were now rolling towards them, dark and ominous. Lightning and thunder, illuminating the sky, promised a heavy downpour.

The moon rose from the east and spread its red glow around, lighting the place like fire. Velan in fact thought that the whole place was on fire, as he sat there in a state of stunned disbelief. Velan's mind raced from Devipattinam to Senthur, for he saw signs of the rain that would bring relief to his village. It was ironic that the rain should come now, within days of his leaving the village. He thought this to be the biggest farce in his life, it was absurd. Even though the moon had dispelled the darkness in the shed, the darkness in Velan's mind could not be dispelled. Muthamma's question, 'Are you going to have some kanji?' startled Velan.

Just then a howling wind blew through the shed, shaking the trees and the thatched structure. Dust swirled into the shed, choking people and settling on the vessels. The flames crackled, scattering sparks of fire everywhere.

'Muthamma! Go get the baby from outside, it is going to rain,' said Velan, as he drank his kanji.

Just as Velan predicted, the rain that had eluded them for so many years, now poured down the skies in torrents. With lightning and thunder, the storm blazed breaking all barriers and shaking the shed as if it would carry the roof away with it. The wind and thunder and lightning, frightened the children.

Darkness filled the shed, and the children clung to their parents. The storm filled the shed with water and the roof threatened to come down on the terrified travellers.

A frightened Valli, buried her face in Velan's lap. There was water everywhere and in the darkness they could not find any place which was dry.

'If it rains like this a few times we will have a good harvest this year,' mused Velan.

'You think one or two rains like this will quench the earth? We should at least have two weeks of rains to slake the parched heart of the earth,' said Muthamma.

'That's true. At least there will be some drinking water for a few days,' said Velan.

'Next year there'll be enough tamarind on the trees and if there's enough water in the pond we might even have some fish,' replied Muthamma in a wistful voice. She could have grown vegetables too. Even thoughts of Sellatha did not excite feelings of dislike or rancour. She thought of her with a kind of yearning and sadness.

'Come Appu, let us go home,' wept Valli. Everyone present there yearned for the same—to return home, to go back to their village.

5

The next morning, the earth was washed clean by the previous day's rains and the sun shone in all its glory in the blue sky. There was a pleasant freshness in the air at Devipatinam, the earth had turned verdant and lush, and puddles of water shimmered as they reflected the sun. Because of the rains they had to begin their journey to Rameswaram in the light of dawn. The storm had left broken branches and uprooted trees in its wake. Watching these sights, they continued walking on the slushy roads, their cracked and bleeding soles soothened and invigorated by the damp soil.

They rested on the way at another ambalam before proceeding to Rameswaram. It was dusk by the time they reached Rameswaram. The children were exhausted, tired and weary.

'I cannot walk any more Appa!' cried Rengan.

'Appa, neither can I,' joined in Suppan.

'Rub some neem oil before you go to sleep. The pain will go away in the morning,' consoled Muthamma.

'Why should we go any further, Ayya? Now that it has rained, let us return home,' said Valli using an adult logic.

Rameswaram was a village near the seashore and instead of the red soil they were used to, they found sandy soil all along the shore. They could see nothing in the inky darkness of the night, but they heard the roaring noise of the thunderous waves lashing against the shore. Since none of them had seen the sea before, their curiosity made them run towards the shore. The milky white rays of the moon was like molten silver on the surface of the sea. They could see the fishing boats and catamarams, with their lights flickering like stars. In the distance, they saw a large ship with its mast hoisted up, tossed about in the sea. A few speculated that they will be going to Ceylon on that big ship.

Although they were bitter about this new life they were venturing into, they felt an excitement in the night air. Everything took on a new glow. They knew their future would have its ups and downs, but they were prepared to face it with courage and fortitude.

There was no rain that night, but the swirling wind beat against the ambalam without respite. This unrest was reflected in the minds of the people who had to spend a sleepless night there.

Many sat through the night, and lit their cooking fires very early in the morning, hoping to warm themselves. Karuppiah Kangany was looking at his books. Velan, unable to sleep, sat through the night, while Valli slept on his lap. Muthamma, tired after the gruelling journey, was fast asleep. The dawn crept in slowly, as the moonlight faded in the horizon. There was a heavenly quiet that had settled there.

The tired and weary travellers woke up from their sleep unwillingly and proceeded with their morning ablutions. Velan wished he could run away from all this, but he was bound by his love for Valli and so much more, that he knew such contemplation was futile.

He did not even notice that Valli had woken up.

'Look, look over there Ayya!' cried Valli in wonder, pointing her finger towards the roof. Velan turned to see what had caught Valli's fancy—through the cracks in the thatched roof he saw the sea and sky converging together in the distance, where the sun was rising in all its glory, shedding its orange red rays. The shells glittered in the sun, the waves aspired to touch the ambalam and receded. This was the scene that caught Valli's attention as she jumped with joy and ran out to pick the shells.

'It looks as if we shall not be able to sail this morning,' said the kangany to the captain of the ship. The ship was actually a large boat with oars and rudders that had to be steered manually.

'The wind is blowing west. It will rip the mast apart. It will be difficult to reach the other shore alive,' feared the Captain.

'Do you think we can sail as soon as the gale subsides?' asked the kangany.

'It will be possible only when the wind changes its course to the east. We can then slowly manage to steer it to the other shore. I think it would take at least another two days for that to happen,' said the captain.

'In that case we have to keep these people here and take care of them. Besides, we have to see that no one runs away, which will be very difficult' said the kangany in frustration.

The people moved hither and thither bringing the place to life. Muthamma gaped in wonder, taking in the scene.

'Did you see that, Muthamma? Did you see what our Valli pointed to us? We are lucky to see all this, aren't we?' said Velan enthusiastically.

'You are the brother-in-law of Saruhani Pandyan, aren't you?' asked a man, approaching Velan.

'Yes! Who are you?" asked Velan.

'I am the one who has married Saruhani Suppan's brother-in-law's daughter. My name is Mookan. I was looking for some company, after all we are all going away to a faraway land. That's why I was looking out for you. Moreover, it is better to keep a distance from the people of my village, they could get one in trouble.'

'How did you know I am Pandyan's brother-in-law?' asked Velan.

'Pandyan himself told me you would be here. But I did not know who you were until I asked a few people and Kakkappan's son directed me to you,' said Mookan.

'Are you on your own?'

'Yes, it is two years since I have been married, my wife is about to have a baby. I thought it would be difficult to take a young girl so far, so I am travelling alone,' said Mookan. He looked very young and handsome, tall with well-built body and broad shoulders. His long thick hair was tied into a knot. His strength echoed in his muscles. His dirt-filled body and clothes did not mar his vitality. He had an affectionate, friendly sparkle in his eyes. Velan took an immediate liking to him.

Valli came running, with her skirt filled with shells and dropped in front of them.

'Is this your daughter?' asked Mookan.

'Yes, and I have another daughter, and two sons. I left my first wife back in the village. I thought it will be difficult to take both my wives to a distant country.'

'Who is this, Ayya?' asked Valli eagerly.

'He is your mama,' introduced Velan.

'Where is he from, Appa?'

'From our village,' said Velan.

'With your family and children, you must be finding it difficult to carry all those bundles. If you need anything I shall be glad to help you. I am alone you see, I am not carrying much,' offered Mookan.

'I wonder why we ever started on this journey. It is raining now, after all these years. That is our luck I must say! Only the god Muniandy is our refuge,' said Velan in a dispirited tone.

'Do you know Kathappan ran away last night? It looks as if they have sent men to fetch him.'

'Do you think anyone would be willing to stay here without being tempted to run away? Already the kangany treats us like cattle and we are not sure of our future. Even I would have run away if I had been on my own,' said Velan.

'What can we do? Wherever we go, we are fated to live like dogs. I am also apprehensive about my future,' said Mookan worriedly.

'Someone told me there is a small shop here. Do you know where it is?' asked Velan.

'It is on the other side of this ambalam. That fellow just about robs you of your money. People say it is better that we take enough kambarisi with us. It is not available in Ceylon. It seems people there don't eat it,' said Mookan.

'Who knows? Only when we reach there will we know! The captain says the winds are strong because it is the month of Aadi. We may have to wait for another two days,' said Velan in a desultory voice.

'Send your son with me, I will get the things you want from the store.'

'Alright, but first I have to get some money from the kangany. I had ten rupees with me when we started out. I have spent it all on betel leaves and other knick knacks,' said Velan, as he and Mookan walked towards the kangany.

'Let me also come with you Ayya,' said Valli, following them.

Muthamma sat staring at the place vacated by them, as she folded the betel leaves and stuffed it into her mouth.

'Renga, go get some sunnambu,' she said, her thoughts returning to the present.

6

Two days had passed since their arrival at Rameswaram. That morning they gathered at the harbour with their things, ready to set sail. A day after their arrival at Rameswaram, they were joined by a throng from Kayalpattinam. Altogether there were more than three hundred to four hundred people who were ready to sail on that ship. There were very few women and children, their number even less than twenty-five.

'They say all of us will have to fit into that ship. It will take at least another fifteen days or so for it to return here, for the next batch. That too depends on the weather conditions,' said a man in the crowd.

'Will there be enough room for all of us in that small ship?' asked Velan shocked.

'We have to somehow get in. Otherwise how will the kangany make money?' said Mookan, sarcastically.

'What difference does it make to poor people like us? Whether we die here or somewhere else, no one is bothered,' said the man in the crowd.

'Hurry up, get into the boat all of you,' shouted the kangany, as he came swinging his umbrella. His face revealed his arrogance and impatience.

A child in the crowd stubbornly refused to get into the boat, weeping and screaming aloud.

'What's going on here? Move, Saniyan! Is it not enough feeding these wretches? I wonder why they have dragged them along,' barked the kangany as he pushed the child with his umbrella, making him tumble to the ground. The child's parents were speechless.

'We will get in, sami,' said the child's father. He was already carrying a child and he wondered how he would carry this one too, when a man in the crowd came to his rescue and said, 'Come child, let me carry you.' Watching this scene, Valli buried her face between her father's legs and began to cry.

'Don't cry, otherwise the kangany ayya will beat you too!' warned Velan, as he carried her on his shoulders.

Not only was the wind blowing strong, but it also began to rain.

The boatmen sang their folk songs as they steered the boat. Their strong and corded muscles shone like bronze in the sunshine.

'Hey, stay by my side, don't get lost in the crowd,' Velan cautioned his son.

Valli began to cry. Afraid of the ship, she refused to get in.

'Chi, you ass! Get up,' said Velan, as he whacked her and carried her screaming to the ship.

'Why are you beating that poor child? What is the harm if we don't go on this journey?' said Muthamma. Seeing Valli cry, the baby too started bawling.

'That's right, let's just stay back and live on the huge fortune you've brought from your father's house,' said Velan annoyed.

'Are you coming or not?' he shouted irritably.

'Let's go, why must we quarrel among ourselves. The kangany is a terrible fellow,' Mookan gently urged them to move. Carrying two bundles and holding the two boys, Suppan and Rengan, he walked ahead. Velan carried the screaming Valli. Muthamma followed them, weeping at their plight.

The people were stuffed in the ship like tamarind pulp. The catamaran was plying back and forth, bringing more and more people into an already overloaded ship. There was no place to move around or even stretch their legs. As the day advanced, it became hotter. Fortunately, the wind brought down the heat, soothing them. But the children drooped and wilted under such conditions.

'When will we reach the other shore?' they asked the captain.

'We should reach before the sun sets,' he said.

People prayed with increased fervour to their family gods. They called aloud for help, at this trying time, when everything seemed so bleak and hopeless.

It drizzled incessantly. The midday heat was brought down by the swirling wind. The angry waves rose higher and higher, dashing against the ship, drenching the people in it. The ship tossed about, like a staggering drunkard.

The captain standing on the masthead shouted, 'Unfurl the mast, the wind has changed its course.' He climbed higher, and the people on the ship were scared that he might fall into the sea, for the wind hurled the ship in different directions. They did not realise that the sailors must have faced many such situations. If they are afraid of this, how could they weather the big storms?

The ship set sail.

The captain shouted out his orders. He was impervious to rain and heat and wind—it was all the same to him. He sat there on the mast, looking at the world, calm and disinterested. How many thousands of such passengers must he have taken on this ship? He was unaffected by their joys and sorrows. His focus was wholly on his ship. He could not be bothered by other things.

The boatmen's song, 'Elelo Ailasa! Elelo Ailasa!' echoed through the ship, as it majestically set sail into the sea. It swayed as it made its way on the high seas. As time went by, the gale strengthened and the clouds darkened, blocking the rays of the sun. It began to rain steadily.

The people on the ship, were shaking with fear. Disjointed reminiscences from their past life, their dreams of striking it rich and returning to their homeland, flitted through their troubled minds. Underneath all this was the foreboding that they may never return to their native land.

'Ele! Lower the mast! The wind has changed direction,' shouted the captain.

'Don't put your heads out. The winds will push you into the sea,' cautioned the kangany. The raging noise of the ocean completely drowned his voice.

Can you imagine the plight of the people on the ship? Caught between the captain and the kangany, the rain and the cold wind, fear and hopelessness, they shivered their way through the journey. They endured the journey without food or water. They reached Ceylon cold and miserable. The journey was not uneventful, they lost two lives, a child who dared to put its head out, and was dragged into the ocean, and a man was struck by a bout of vomiting and diarrhoea. He died of dehydration. His corpse was tossed into the ocean. The people on the boat lost the little hope that had lurked in the corner of their hearts. Everything turned into a mirage.

'Only our gods can save us.' This was the conclusion they had come to, as they prayed fervently for protection. It was only when they saw the shores of Ceylon, that they felt life slowly ebb back into their terrified souls.

Valli was shrivelled and almost lifeless from lack of food or water. Her throat was parched, it was impossible for her to speak. She fainted often on the ship, which made Velan fear for her life. Muthamma was so weak, she could neither weep nor comfort her children. It was a miracle really that Velan's family reached the other shore in safety. Mookan too survived the journey.

'Valli my child, here drink some water. Open your eyes, look at us!' Velan forced some water through her locked jaws and tried to resuscitate her. On reaching the shore they lit a fire and warmed her feet. Slowly, she came back to life.

Velan was so relieved, he burst into tears. 'My darling, why did I put you through this journey? God, nothing must happen to my child,' he pleaded aloud. Muthamma, drained of energy and emotions, sat frozen like a stone. She had never seen Velan weep like this before, she was surprised and shocked to see him in this state. Mookan also felt sympathy for the desolate Velan.

'Vela, don't worry. Our god will protect us, Valli will get better. Come, let us go to the ambalam and make arrangements for food and water. That will help her recover.' Mookan gently led them to the ambalam, where he lit a fire and started cooking. Not heeding his own exhaustion he was engrossed in taking care of Velan's family.

Velan, crazed with sorrow, sat in a corner of the ambalam. He gazed at the sea with its restless waves crashing against the shore. It reminded him of the futility of his own life. He felt powerless against the strong tides of fate.

The storm had subsided, the rain had ceased and the sun was out.

'Do you know where we are now?' asked Mookan.

Ignoring Mookan's query, looking at the recovering Valli, Velan said, 'Let Valli gain strength, we shall then return to our own village.'

'Vela, have no fear. I am here for you. Valli will come to no harm. It is all because of starvation and hunger. Once you feed her and also have some food yourself, everything will be alright and life will look brighter,' said Mookan.

Velan realised the truth in his argument.

'Do you know the name of this place? It's called Pesalai, we are now in Ceylon. People say it will take at least four or five days to reach the hill town, which is our destination.'

On hearing this, Velan's spirit plummeted to new depths. 'What did you say? Walk some more? Do you think our children will be able to take any more of this?' Velan was incensed by this bit of news.

'We've got to proceed, even if we have to carry them ourselves. Having come all this way where can we go now?' reasoned Mookan.

'I cannot walk any further. I can hardly move!' wept Muthamma.

'Let's hope for the best,' said Velan.

They did not have a choice. The kangany nudged and prodded, until he got them all to move. He herded them along like sheep and cattle, totally unconcerned by their state.

'What do you think this is? A charitable institution? Get up, it is getting late! If you were looking for a good time, you should have stayed at home and slept comfortably,' declared the kangany, bullying them along to their destination.

After passing some Sinhalese villages, they reached Pannamam with great difficulty. At Pannamam, a white man took count of them and left.

Velan was even more dejected, when the baby Papathi died of diarrhoea on the way. Muthamma thought it was for the best. Velan was wild with fury, blaming himself for the folly of embarking on this journey.

'If you put your foot in the mud, prepare to get soiled,' quoted Mookan.

'Let it go, they will only earn our curses. We've been had before.' Muthamma cursed, even as she shivered with the malarial fever that had taken hold of her. She had grown weak and emaciated, losing the little strength she had. Valli had become skeletal.

At last they reached Nawalapitiya. It had taken them more than ten days to reach this hill town.

7

Hamilton Estate, their final destination, was seven miles from Nawalapitiya.

'Here we are, at last we have arrived! This is our estate!' said the kangany, puffing with pride.

All along the way they had seen people like themselves, who had come from India, clearing and burning jungles, planting coffee and tea seedlings.

'Is it all coffee in this estate?' asked one man curiously.

'No, we have also some tea bushes,' said the kangany. They reached a massive iron gate that was locked. Seeing the crowd, a watchman came up to the gate from a nearby shed.

'Hey! Open the gate,' the kangany called out.

'Come in kangany ayya, come in,' the watchman welcomed the kangany with a smile spread across his face. The gate opened with a loud screeching noise, and after all of them went through, it was locked again with a decisive clang. The kangany turned around and checked if all of them had entered the estate and no one was left behind.

'Are the dorai and others keeping well?' asked the kangany.

'They are all fine, ayya,' replied the watchman.

'Go on, keep moving,' said the kangany as he hustled them.

They felt like they were being led into a prison. Bereft of human activity, a frightening silence pervaded the estate, chilling their souls. With heavy hearts, they slowly dragged themselves up the hill.

They looked around them and saw that on one side was the virgin forest, and that the other side had been cleared and coffee bushes were planted neatly in rows.

As they climbed higher, it got bitterly cold and the wind pierced their half-naked bodies like sharp needles. The gravel on the pathway pierced their soles, making them bleed. As they reached the summit they could see nothing, for the mist covered the whole place like a white sheet.

As the mist cleared, they saw a frothing waterfall, rushing out of the crevices of a hill and forming a river that flowed through the plantation.

'I would love to go down and bathe in that water!' said Velan, enthralled by the sight.

'In this cold?' asked Mookan, astonished.

'If not for the cold, I would be in that water by now,' Velan said, looking wistfully at the waterfall.

As they walked down the slope, they saw a beautiful wooden building before them. The kangany went in. He came out in a short while, accompanied by a big, burly white man, who reminded them of the man they had seen at Pannamam. But this man was quite different from him. This man was fat and short, with flesh hanging down from his cheeks. He looked like an overripe watermelon—ugly, florid and comical. He had a hard, sour face, churlish and mean. He was dressed like other white men, in ubiquitous khaki shorts, shirt and a topi. He took stock of them with cold eyes, and walked away, down the slope.

'Come, let me take you all to the layyam,' beckoned the kangany's man.

They were led to a place with a cluster of shacks. A couple of people came out to watch them.

Velan asked the man who was leading them, 'No one seems to be here, where is everyone?'

'They must have all gone to work. These people must have stayed behind,' he replied.

'Let these newcomers stay here until they build their own layyam,' said the kangany.

'Alright,' said the man nodding in agreement.

'Ask them to buy anything they want from the store. Tell them they have got to report to work at the first siren call,' instructed the kangany, as he left them.

The exhausted and tired travellers were beyond thinking. They just wanted to curl up and sleep, even though the sheds were cold, damp and smelly.

As the sun went down, darkness shrouded the plantation. The dewdrops nestling on the tea and coffee plants shimmered like diamonds. There was a verdant lushness all around them.

It was a scene that could have refreshed the heart of any onlooker. But to those who had just arrived, it meant nothing, as they were numbed by exhaustion.

A woman from the neighbouring room in the layyam came in, bringing a tin lamp. 'Here, take this lamp. What will you do in the dark?' She offered the lamp to Muthamma.

'This child is very sick, I wish I could make some kanji for her,' said Muthamma.

'I will bring some kanji. My name is Sivakami, I live next door. If you need anything, just call me.'

Valli's tender body was burning with a fever which made her restless and delirious.

In that musty room, the mosquitoes and fleas bothered them all night, making it impossible to sleep. The cold wind pierced their bones, making them shiver.

Exhausted by the journey, unable to keep an attentive vigil on the sick child, Velan would drift away into sleep, only to be rudely awakened by the persistent mosquitoes.

Before dawn broke, they heard the siren call summoning them to work.

'Wake up, we have to be at the roll-call shed before the next siren call,' said Sivakami, as she woke them up.

'This child is very sick. I am not going to work today. He alone will go,' said Muthamma, pointing to Velan and huddling under her blanket.

At the shed, they saw another man, wearing a long coat and turban, waiting with the kangany.

'He is the kanakapillai,' whispered Mookan.

The kangany and the other man sat down at their table and started looking through some books.

'Hey! Raise the wick in the lantern, I can hardly see anything,' said the kangany to his assistant. As the wick was raised, the flame in the lantern flickered to life. The lantern looked as if it had not been cleaned in a very long time, and a weak light filtered through the glass. It reflected the inner reality of the newcomers who had made the journey hoping for a new life. Their hearts too flailed and flagged like the lamp.

The sun slowly crept through the mist and the clouds. The resounding clap of horse's hooves broke the silence of the morning.

'The dorai is coming,' someone alerted them.

Getting off his horse, swishing his whip, the dorai walked in. The kangany and the kanakapillai stood up meekly.

The dorai glanced at them haughtily, and proceeded to look at the books.

'How many workers have come?' asked the dorai.

'Three hundred, sir.'

'Do they need new layyam?'

'Yes, dorai.'

'Alright, let us see what can be done,' said the dorai dismissively, as he left.

'You have to build your own layyam. I will ask permission from the dorai and give you the necessary wood and other materials.'

'Yes, ayya,' said the men.

'The new men will have to cut and clear the jungle for now,' said the kangany's assistant.

'Alright, let them do that,' said the kangany sternly. In the dim morning light the kangany's face was like a carved stone, showing no emotion. His vulture eyes pierced through the workers, looking into their souls.

It took them some time to construct their layyam. Velan's family had to face extreme discomfort until they were assigned their own room. It took many weeks for Muthamma and Valli to recover from their illness.

In the evenings, the workers got together to talk about the villages they had left behind. The biting cold and vicious mosquitoes made their nights miserable.

Muthamma was indifferent to the life on the estate—it neither excited nor bothered her. She longed to go back to her village, as she believed starvation was better than exile. Time healed this craving as they gradually came to accept their life on the estate.

The jungles were cut down to make way for tea and coffee plantations. The workers watched their labour take root, grow and flourish. But their lives, so hopelessly intertwined with the plantation, did not share the same fecundity. Unable to resist the vagaries of fate, their bodies and souls felt deadened by their burdens. Velan's family was not an exception—their hopes too had shrivelled up like the wilting petals of a rose. They too became used to the strange ways of plantation life.

'Atha, are there many white men like our dorai?' asked the curious Valli.

'Yes, there are many like him in this country,' replied Muthamma.

Muthamma was sometimes puzzled by her neighbour Sivakami's behaviour. She noticed her behaving in a very familiar manner with the kangany and the kanakapillai—talking and laughing behind the tea and coffee bushes.

'Did you see that?' asked Muthamma, furtively.

'See what?' asked Velan, playing dumb.

'The next door woman, Sivakami.'

'What about her?'

'What do you mean? Did you not see the way she talked to the kangany?'

'To whom the woman talks to is not your concern.'

'Don't you have eyes? Can't you see what's before you? No wonder people take you for a ride so easily,' she berated him, as she popped the betel and tobacco into her mouth.

'Let it be. We cannot get involved in all that. Anyone can drink the water in the river, it is free you know? You don't have to pay for it,' Velan guffawed at his own joke.

For a moment Velan visualised Sivakami—her slender body, the sinuous walk, the ripe well-rounded breasts that kept pace with the bounce in her step, her tightly wrapped sari, the tinkling thandai, the dangling earrings, her wistful talk, her provocative laugh. All these, compounded with her youth, was heady stuff—Velan thought no man can help but desire her.

Velan had often seen the lust-filled eyes of the kangany devouring her. The kanakapillai too often stood there, his eyes feasting on her, his swelling groin seeking satisfaction. The people in the plantation were well aware of this situation.

'That lame fellow is not fit to be her husband. She belongs to the bedroom with soft mattresses,' Velan had heard the kanakapillai mutter under his breath.

But Sivakami was well aware of her assets—her seductive body and enticing looks. She also knew that it was all she had, and knew how to capitalise on them.

She would make the men around her hot and bothered and slowly sweep her eyes over the dorai with an easy smile. She would flutter her eyelids and tighten her sari, bringing his attention to her luscious breasts. It was not as if the dorai was impervious to her tactics. His blood-shot eyes filled with desire, and his swelling shorts were an unspoken testament.

Even though Velan was amused by her games, some nights he had a hard time sleeping. He was aware that Sivakami was just next door. On these nights he turned to Muthamma, who had to forgo her sleep.

The usually silent Velan burst out one day. 'That good-for-nothing fellow does not know how to keep his wife happy. He has let her run wild, grazing where she pleases!'

'I cannot stomach this. I wish we had stayed back home, with our dignity and morals intact,' said Muthamma.

'At least we are getting a meal here,' said Velan.

Mookan walked in, carrying an axe in one hand and a wild boar in the other. 'Looks like our Queen Sivakami rules,' he said mockingly.

'Come in Mooka, we were just talking about her,' said Velan.

'In our next birth we would be lucky to have a life like hers. Look at this boar. Isn't she a beauty! We found her while clearing the forest down the slope. We had a tough time getting this one, she was all set to tear Ponnan to pieces.'

'It looks like a fat one.'

'It was quite a job carrying this one up here. It was then that we saw the queen talking to...' said Mookan with a sneer.

'I don't think we should be talking about this. Give me that axe and I will chop up this boar,' said Velan.

8

Muthamma gradually recovered, and started working on the estate. She was not completely fit enough to work, she had lost a lot of weight and looked thin and wan.

During the coffee season, the women picked coffee berries and at other times, they cut grass. The men had to clear the jungles, prune the coffee and tea bushes and fertilize the soil.

The jungles were ancient and magnificent—they were not like the barren, dry land they had left, nor like the thorny acacia covered woods they had seen on their journey. These forests were filled with wild animals and giant trees interwined with vines, closely knit and dense. During the rainy season they became mosquito-infested swamps. People wanting to stay alive would not dare enter this jungle. But braving these conditions the coolies brought the tea and coffee plantations into existence. During the nights, they had a watchman beating on a tin drum, and a big roaring fire to keep away the wild animals.

Ironically, the people working in these estates did not fear the wild animals or the mosquitoes, they only feared their bosses.

One morning, Muthamma woke up early as usual, and walked to the roll-call shed. The bitter cold hit her with a vengeance, making her teeth chatter. She pulled a thin blanket around her shoulders, trying in vain to warm her numbed fingers.

The ground was slippery and she could not walk fast. It was not just her body, but her hopes too had frozen.

Why should they live in this miserable cold and rain, she thought with bitterness. Why were they fated to live this life, and what was its purpose? Nothing made sense anymore. The overhanging mist covering the pathway made it risky for her to walk fast, if she missed her footing she knew she would fall down the precipice.

Tearing the silence of the cold morning, Muthamma heard a man's voice.

'Sivakami, you will come without fail, won't you? I will be waiting by our tree for you. Come soon, don't make me wait!'

'Yes, wait for me. I will be there, as soon as I can,' whispered the woman's voice in the dark. Muthamma had no doubt that it was Sivakami's voice.

'Alright! You go to the roll-call shed. I will meet you later,' bade the kangany, climbing up a slope. Muthamma hurriedly hid behind a bush.

Muthamma saw Sivakami walk towards the roll-call shed. She followed her, keeping her distance. She did not know that Sivakami was this familiar with the kangany. It made her uncomfortable, and she told herself, 'Wherever you go, your sins follow you'. They had left Senthur, hoping to lead a life with self-respect and dignity. Enduring the cold and the rain, they were trying to make a life for themselves. Unfortunately, it now became clear that they would never be allowed to have a peaceful and simple existence. She did not blame Sivakami. She only blamed the life they had been led to.

A few months after this incident, one morning, the kanakapillai waylaid her and said, 'Muthamma, today you have to work down in the lower fields, cutting the grass.'

This was the season when the coffee berries ripened and women went to pick them. Surprised, she wondered why he should ask her to cut grass, but since she could not refuse or go against his orders she went down to the field where he had asked her to work. The rain had made the ground slushy and it was infested with leeches. She took her tobacco pouch and pressed the tobacco on her bleeding legs to remove the leeches. As she prepared to cut the grass, she saw the kanakapillai climb down from the upper slope. The dew drops on the grass shone like little silver beads. With the exertion of work, she felt a warmth creeping up her chilled body.

'Hey woman, are the leeches troubling you?' the kanakapillai asked, as he climbed down with his umbrella.

'There will always be plenty of leeches in the wet grass,' said Muthamma dismissively, as she continued working.

'Are you feeling better now? Are you taking the tablets that the dorai gave you?' he asked her, as if he was truly concerned. It only irritated her.

'I am alright,' she answered tersely.

'Why are you so sullen? I asked you because I wanted to help you. Don't be so curt,' said the kanakapillai, as he sidled closer to her. She removed herself to a distance and looked at him with anger and distaste.

'Hey, why are you looking at me like that? You have come so far with your family and children, and I see you struggling so much. I thought I would help you. I could not offer anything in front of those useless fellows, that is why I came down here to talk to you, alone.' In one stride he closed the space between them and was beside her.

'People do things for a reason. There is a price to be paid for everything,' Muthamma said as she tried to move away from him.

When she saw the kanakapillai persisting in his attempts to seduce her, she burst out angrily, 'Stay away from me! I don't want you coming here offering your sympathy. I know all about men like you!'

'Come on Muthamma, I see you having a hard time with your children and your ill health and I thought I could help you out. Give you some money, maybe,' he said.

'What? You want to give me money? That too from the kindness of your heart, that's funny. You don't give us the wages we legitimately deserve! Chi! Have you no shame? You pick on poor people like us. You don't even have the honour and dignity that we poor have. Get away from here!' she said, raising her hoe threateningly.

'Look at her! She talks as if she is the goddess of chastity. She looks like a harmless kitten, but there is no end to her loud mouth. Serves me right for trying to help a bitch like you. You trash! You don't realise whom you are talking to!' ranted the kanakapillai, as he hurried away from the place. Muthamma was furious, and at the same time she feared the repercussions of this incident. After a while she resigned herself to her fate and was resolved to take things in her stride.

'May he go straight to hell! Let the devil take him! Let our god Muniyandi give him his dues!' she cursed under her breath, spat on the direction in which the kanakapillai had left, and got on with her work.

She did not talk about this incident to anyone, not even Velan, for fear of a confrontation. Burying it inside her mind, she grimly waited for the reprisal. Even though the kanakapillai did not say anything to her after that, she felt his hawk-like eyes boring into her, ready to burn her to ashes.

'Muthamma, your work seems to slacken day by day. If you don't do your work properly, what do you think we should do?' derided the kanakapillai, in a loud voice, for everyone to hear.

'From now on I will do as you say, ayya,' she said meekly. She knew there was no use antagonising him. She also knew nothing good would come out of it. She had her family and children to think of, she had to give in gracefully. She hated the disgusting, hateful life she was forced to lead. She hopelessly searched for a way out, but her efforts were in vain. Muthamma was not the only one. All the labourers in the plantation shared a similar plight.

'Muthamma, why are you still standing here? Are you not going to work today?' asked Sivakami, as they dispersed from the roll-call shed.

'Muthamma and her husband would love to get paid for not working. It pains them to work! Go, go to work all of you!' shouted the kangany. Everyone headed for the slopes and Muthamma followed them.

9

'Muthamma, where is Mookan?' asked Velan, as he walked in.

Muthamma was seated by the doorway, wrapped in a blanket, with her legs outstretched as she chewed her betel leaves and tobacco. Suppan was chopping firewood, Valli was washing the cooking pots and pans. The younger boy Rengan was cleaning the tapioca for dinner.

'He just left looking for Kakkan. Kakkan had come from India yesterday. He wanted to find out if there was any news from home.'

'They were talking about it in the field. They said sixty new men have come from India. Valli, get me some tobacco. Renga, go to the store and get some rice. I am tired of eating jackfruit and tapioca everyday,' said Velan, as he warmed himself by the kitchen fire.

'Ayya, shall I get you some coffee?' asked Valli.

'Yes, it would be nice to have something hot. It has been extremely cold today. Even though we are at the end of Masi, it's still cold.'

Muthamma called out to Velan.

'What is it?' he asked.

'Nothing...hmm, did you send any money home?'

'How is that possible? Some time ago the kanakapillai said he had sent some money. He told me the other day that I have too much debt in my account and he will not be able to give me any more loans or send any money home,' Velan said in a tired voice.

'From the time we came here, he has been saying the same thing. I wonder when we will ever be free of all this.'

'Here ayya, coffee...' said Valli, offering it to Velan.

'Has Velan come back from work?' asked Mookan, as he entered their dwelling.

'Come in, Mooka. It is very cold outside, come here and warm your hands by the fire,' invited Velan.

'Yes, it has been extremely cold, especially in the higher ranges. I went to see Kakkan. My wife has sent some murukku and some oil, I went to fetch them. Here, Valli, take these. My god, how cold it is! Kakkan's layyam is like a fowl shed, there are seven or eight men in one room. I wonder how they manage,' said Mookan, as he joined Velan by the fire.

'Did you ask about the rains and harvest back home? Have they had good rains in Senthur?' asked Velan eagerly. His eyes misted when he thought of his village.

'Sellatha wants to get your son Maruthai married. She wants you to send some money. Poor woman, she does not know our difficulties. Valli, give me some water,' said Mookan. Valli brought coffee and gave it to him.

'I will have to go somehow. It must be more than four years since we came here. I wonder how she is. Last year I asked if I could go for a visit, the kangany said I'll have to pay all my debts before I go. I wonder what he is going to say this year,' said Velan, distressed by the circumstances.

'What else is he going to say? He will say the same thing. Anyway ask him for whatever it is worth. Since you will be leaving the family behind, he may agree. Otherwise he might think you will go there and stay for good. He will not send you.'

'I wonder how they are back home. Let us all go!' said Muthamma.

'That's right, we have all the wealth in the world, you see, we can all go for a visit now! You are such a fool. Have you forgotten how difficult our journey to Ceylon was? Can you imagine doing it again, dragging these children along? At least if we had some land in the village, I would have tried to send these boys. Let us see what can be done. So how was the harvest this year?' asked Velan, once again.

'The harvest was alright. My brother-in-law, they say, died last year and my wife is managing on her own. If not for the child I could ask her to come here. But with these fellows, who knows what humiliations she may have to put up with?'

'It was our fate that it was always famine and drought, all the time we were there. Otherwise why would we come to this godforsaken country. At least after we came here there has been rain and good fortune for our people,' Velan said dejectedly.

'At least you try to go,' said Muthamma, realising Velan's frustration.

'Ayya, the kanakapillai refused to give rice at the store. He said something about our debts piling up,' said Rengan, returning from the store.

Hearing this Velan was enraged. In Senthur, even while working for the mirasdar, he had never felt so humiliated or insulted. From the time he came here, he had to put up with a lot of abuse from the kangany, the kanakapillai, the dorai and the rest. Although they slaved all day they never saw the fruits of their labour. If they demanded their pay, they were easily fobbed off with, 'You have debts to pay.' They were kept half-hungry and desperate. This seemed to be the kangany and kanakapillai's strategy. Velan felt rage and resentment building up inside him—he wanted to use his pruning knife and seek his revenge.

'Scoundrels, did he refuse to give you rice? Wait, I will go now and finish him off with this pruning knife!' said Velan outraged.

'Don't do anything like that. Your anger will not affect them in any way. They will join together and see that you are cut up in pieces. Go tomorrow and ask him in a nice manner and see what he says,' advised Mookan, restraining the incensed Velan.

'Yes, he is right. Already those fellows are irked by us, and are waiting for an opportunity to flex their muscles. They wouldn't hesitate to butcher us,' Muthamma said, with fear in her voice. She knew the reason for the kanakapillai's resentment towards them. But how could she tell the truth to Velan? He would be even more angered.

'How can we live like this for the rest of our lives—without self-respect and dignity? We work like dogs, and are treated like dogs. Is that why he brought us here? Let me go ask him!' Velan was furious.

'Why invite trouble? If you were on your own it wouldn't matter, but you have a family to think of,' Mookan cautioned him once again.

'Let it rest, our Muniyandi will take care of them. I am biding my time,' said Muthamma, with tears welling up in her eyes.

For a while there was an eerie silence in the room, only the sparks flying from the burning firewood and the bubbling of boiling water broke the silence.

'Vela, did you hear the news? Last year the coffee plants were affected by bugs, which was a loss for them. So this year they are planting tea, even in the lower fields. The newly cleared land is also for tea,' said Mookan.

'Let them all go to hell! Who cares what they do, as long as they give us our wages,' replied Velan.

'It seems they are also going to get another dorai from England. The junior kanakapillai was talking about it at the office.'

'Our dorai needs more help, I suppose. He gets cartons and cartons of liquor from England, gets drunk and rolls on the ground all day,' said Mookan.

'It is not just the alcohol. The kangany fellow brings all kinds of sleazy women for him,' said Muthamma.

'Ayya, there is a path down the lower slope that the kangany uses to quietly sneak in and out of the estate,' said Suppan, who had been listening to the conversation.

Velan and the rest looked at him surprised. It suddenly dawned on them that Suppan was no longer a child. He had grown into a tall, handsome young man. 'He has become old enough to start working,' Velan thought to himself. He asked him, 'How do you know this?'

'The other day when I went to bring firewood I saw the pathway. He has a watchman there, to make sure no one leaves the estate. The watchman goes to the village, returns dead drunk and sleeps it off. He wouldn't know if anyone goes or comes into the estate.'

'Is that how you manage to bring in all that jackfruit?' questioned Velan.

'I don't think he knows what he's saying,' said Mookan.

'Alright, alright, but don't mess around with these fellows. They can get rid of you without a trace,' warned Mookan.

'They wouldn't dare touch me. Let them try, I will slaughter them with this pruning knife. I am not like my father,' said Suppan with much bravado.

'The boy really has grown up,' Velan thought in wonder. 'Alright, alright, but we don't want unnecessary trouble,' Velan said aloud.

'I would have finished them off the other day itself, but thinking of atha and the rest of you, I let them be,' Suppan said with a swagger.

'Hey, listen you fellow, don't you create any more trouble than we already have. Understand?' admonished Muthamma.

Secretly she was pleased that her son has now grown into a plucky young man. At the same time a nameless fear made her uneasy. Just then Rengan walked into the layyam. In the enshrouding darkness, with just a faint light thrown by a lamp, he too looked all grown up—with long, luxuriant hair, dark body like polished ebony, broad forehead and large eyes. He threw his axe down in a corner and said, 'I am going for a bath.'

'Come, I am also going to the river to fetch some water,' said Suppan. Both went out together.

'The boys have grown up. It will be good if they too get jobs,' murmured Muthamma.

'Do you want them also to die like us everyday? It would be nice if we could send them back home and set them up with some farm land.'

'That would be wonderful,' replied Muthamma.

10

Velan was standing in front of his layyam, lost in thought. Ever since he had received the message from home, he was homesick and wanted to go back to India.

'Hey Vela, why haven't you gone to work?' asked the kanakapillai.

'They told me at the store that they will not give us rice. If you could only tell them to give me some rice and dry fish...' said Velan, meekly. He glanced sideways and saw that the dorai was in the vicinity.

'If you keep borrowing, what can we do? We cannot keep giving, can we? Because you have wife and children, what you earn is not enough. You have to do something about it. What can we do?' said the kanakapillai.

'Where can we go, sami? If we can't make a living here then we'll have to return to our village. Why don't you settle our accounts and give us something, we will be glad to return to India. We came here trusting you, and its been almost three years now, and we haven't gone home, even once. I have another wife and children there. I just heard they too are dying of starvation. If I go back home for good, somehow I will manage...' Velan said piteously.

'Oh, so you have planned to go back home, have you? Well, what about the loan taken from the kangany? You have not even paid the interest for it. Besides, what about the money you often borrow and send home, who is to repay that? You better find a way of paying up all your debts before you think of returning to India, is that clear?' said the kanakapillai. The dorai and the kangany came out and listened to the conversation.

'What's going on here?' asked the kangany in an authoritative voice.

'This fellow wants to go back home, I told him to clear all his debts before thinking of returning home,' said the kanakapillai, as he shook his head disapprovingly.

The dorai whispered something to the kangany and left the place, riding away on his horse.

'What's your problem, Vela? All these people here are not anxious to go home, so why are you so keen? At least they do their work properly! You don't even do that, but you want to go back home, leaving a whole lot of debts behind,' the kangany chastised him.

'No, no, ayya, it is not that! It's just that it's been more than three years since I came here. There is another wife and family back home. I thought it's about time I saw them again. I will leave Muthamma and the children here on the estate,' he said in a conciliatory manner. He knew this was not the place to exhibit his anger for it would only make things worse for him and his family.

'Fine! Just settle your account before you think of going home.'

'But ayya, if you refuse to give rice on our account we will starve. Then how can we work?'

'Alright, you can go now. Try to buy less on your account from now on, understand?'

'Ayya, he has not even paid for the blankets he had bought for his family so far,' said the kanakapillai, not wanting to make things easy for Velan.

'Check how many blankets, will you?'

The kanakapillai made a pretence of looking at his ledger and arriving at his calculations. His pock-marked, whiskered face looked disfigured and repulsive. Climbing up and down the hills had given him a sturdy physique, but he had no height. In spite of not running to fat, he looked like a waddling duck. Bending down and looking through his books, he presented a comic picture.

'Why is it taking so long? Look quickly and tell me. It's time he got to work, how long do you think he can hang around here?' said the kangany, irritated by the delay.

'If he comes at the time of roll-call and breathes down my neck, what can I do? With more than three hundred workers to be attended to, I cannot drop everything to deal with him alone,' said the kanakapillai with resentment.

'If you wish I will come in the evening after I finish work,' said Velan.

'Just wait. Do you think I have no other work, that I have to attend to you now and once again in the evening? Hmm...let's see, three white blankets and two black blankets—a total of five blankets in your account,' said the Kanakapillai.

Velan knew very well that they would deduct at least a year's wages for the white and black blankets. Besides, this blanket account had stretched on for so many years, with the interest adding on remorselessly to the principal. Velan let his raised vetti down and walked out saying, 'Please do whatever you can. I will be happy if my family does not go hungry.'

'Alright! Go now, go and do your work properly. We will see what can be done later,' said the kangany, as if they had quarrelled and he was settling the dispute.

'What did the periya kangany say?' asked Mookan.

'What is there to say? He is not going to say anything new today, it is the same old story.'

'I know, but if we let those gods have their way, like our queen Sivakami does, then they would show some mercy and grant you your wishes,' said Kakkan derisively, twirling his pruning knife. Everyone laughed, except Velan who was not amused.

'Not everyone can be like that lame cuckold, without shame or self-respect,' Velan said angrily.

'Shame and self-respect? You have to bundle all that up and set it aside if you wish to survive here. You are a fool. Can you hold on to your self-respect if you wish to send money home, or buy lands, or even build houses back home?' asked Kakkan, his words dripping with sarcasm. Kakkan was considered something of a clown among them. Whenever someone felt low, he said something to make them laugh, which eased the situation.

'You are another one, you just succeed in giving me a heartburn!' said Velan.

'Hey, why are you so bothered? After all, we live today and die tomorrow! What do you think will happen if we fall down this precipice? Supposing in the night a fox kills us—who is there to ask about us? Supposing the kangany or the dorai assault us and bury us under the bushes, who is there to question them? You talk as if you are going to live for a hundred years! As long as you are innocent, you don't have to worry unnecessarily,' said Kakkan philosophically. Everyone stopped their work for a moment and enjoyed his sermon.

'You are a fine one to talk! You have left behind your wife and children, and lead a carefree life here,' said Mookan.

'Yes, carefree life indeed! I might even die today, who knows? Why should I worry about anything? Am I supporting my wife and children? Or, am I sending them pots of money, like I promised to? Somehow they are surviving and I too am keeping my body and soul together. Why should we worry about this?' said Kakkan, his words echoing in that coffee plantation. Everyone agreed that there was truth in what he said.

They saw the kangany approaching and got back to work.

That evening Velan reflected on what Kakkan had said, as he chewed his betel leaves. He tried to understand why he could not be free of all this anxiety. If only Muthamma did not take life so seriously and had 'compromised' a little, all these troubles would have disappeared long ago. Muthamma was lying in a corner, on an old torn mat, wrapped in blankets. Velan heard the faint sound of her breathing intermingled with the buzz of the mosquitoes. They bit her uncovered face and drew blood wherever they could. Her emaciated face, thin and wan, looked like that of a ghost. She breathed with her mouth slightly open. Betel juice trickled down from her mouth like blood. Troubles and travails and illness had completely transformed her. Suddenly he felt a revulsion for her. He thought of Sivakami in the neighbouring room—her curvaceous figure, her sparkling eyes, her sinuous walk. There was simply no comparison between them. He suddenly felt sorry for Muthamma.

Was Kakkan right? Could he afford to live only in the present? Then what happens to Valli? What about Suppan and Rengan's futures? He could not find the answers for these questions.

11

Valli was now ten years old. She had grown taller and started wearing long skirts. She would groom her hair with a broken wooden comb, and tie it up in a bun. Like her mother, she had a quiet calmness in her eyes; at the same time there was an air of liveliness about her. She was smart and bright and did her work with enthusiasm. Her broad forehead, large black eyes, sharp nose and round face were charming, and even in that young age she was endowed with a certain grace. Even though she was just ten, the constant company of adults, and sharing this strange, desolate life with them, had made her mature beyond her years. Totally isolated from the outside world, the labourers led unambitious lives. They were simple, honest, warmly affectionate and always polite and respectful. They were seldom arrogant, jealous or violent. Living among them, Valli imbibed their mannerisms and began to behave like them. She would help herself to her mother's betel leaves, gossip with the neighbours, and share the stories with her parents when they return home from work.

The boys Suppan and Rengan too took the cue from their father and set their minds on working hard.

In this manner, Velan's family slowly got on with their lives over the years. Muthamma conceived once again. Her already weak constitution made it difficult for her to trudge up and down the mountains, in her condition. Having no choice, she continued working, exposing herself to the rain and the sun.

'The river is in spate, the water is murky,' said Valli, as she walked in with the water pot.

'Somewhere up in the mountains, it must have rained heavily,' said Velan.

'Plenty of firewood is drifting down the river, but the currents are strong, we cannot get to it,' said Rengan.

'Well, don't go near the water collecting firewood. We sometimes have flash floods,' warned Muthamma.

'They have to be prepared to deal with everything. If you bring them up like this, how will they manage? They have to watch out for the floods and get away in time. The water will wash down big logs to the banks, that should tide us over for the rainy season, which will soon begin. Suppa, you go along with Rengan and help him get the firewood,' said Velan.

'I can't go now. In this dark who will go and pick firewood? If you wish I will go in the morning. With the mist closing in, we won't be able to see the path,' said Suppan

'Why don't you light a flare and go, instead of talking big like a dorai!' Velan said, irritated with his son.

'How can he go in this dark night and miserable cold. It's freezing, you can't put your hands in the water,' said Muthamma.

'Alright, he just wants to go to the village tomorrow under the pretext of gathering firewood, that's why he's making these excuses,' said Velan.

'No ayya, the water is really cold. Even as I was walking up the hill it was growing dark and I could hardly see the pathway,' Valli defended her brother.

It was indeed pitch dark outside, with heavy fog completely annihilating the weak rays of the evening sun. From the mountain slopes they could see the last rays of the sun splayed out in a riot of colours in the fields below. Patches of blue sky were revealed in the midst of a black cloud cover—two stars blossomed in this magical strip of blue. 'Valli, get me some hot water,' said Velan.

'I think we are in for a cold spell,' said Muthamma, as she warmed herself in front of the stove, wrapped in a blanket. She sat chewing betel leaves in the warmth. Valli, mindful of her mother's delicate health, willingly took over the responsibility of running the house. There were no miracles lighting up their dreary lives. But one or two changes that took place did affect their lives in various ways.

A new dorai arrived at the plantation. The number of workers on the estate too increased with time. More and more forests were cleared, and prepared for the tea bushes. The air was filled with the fragrance of tender green tea saplings.

The new dorai was very young and had no prior knowledge of plantation work. He had amazingly beautiful blue eyes. They were not like the cat-like grey eyes of the big dorai, which were frightening at times, especially when he was drunk. When the new dorai stood tall with his white shirt and khaki breeches, his hair shone like the golden straw in the fields. Some naive labourers even wondered if he had cut the straw and pasted it on his head. He took his work seriously and attended to it with interest. He always had a smile on his lips.

They called him the sinna dorai, and they found that he was quite different from the old periya dorai. The older man was always impatient and yelled at them indiscriminately, whereas the sinna dorai would patiently look into every detail with care and interest. But sometimes he too exhibited the same haughty indifference while dealing with the workers. Was it because of their black skin? Were they therefore nothing more than animals? Or was it because he did not wish to get too familiar with the dark-skinned labourers? Or did he fear the displeasure of the periya dorai? In spite of this, the labourers liked him, even while they respected and feared him.

'Vela, there has been another message from home for you. Your first wife wants you to come home to get your son married,' Kakkan told Velan while they were at work.

'Do you think I can go for a wedding now? The marriage will definitely take place whether I go or not. I am not prepared to beg those fellows and be humiliated again,' said Velan.

'Our sinna dorai is different. Why don't you ask him?'

'Let's see, after all they are all of the same colour,' said Velan. Just then they heard a small commotion, down the slopes, where the women were working. It caught everyone's attention.

'What's up? What's happening here?' The kanakapillai came down the slope demanding an explanation.

'Sivakami has fainted, and it looks like she's having fits,' said a woman in the crowd.

'What? Did you say fits? Let's see...' said the kanakapillai, as he rushed to look into the problem. A very pregnant Sivakami was lying on the ground, her mouth frothing and contorted, eyeballs pulled upwards, her limbs caught in unceasing convulsions. The kanakapillai was alarmed.

'Come on all of you, give a hand. Let's carry her to the coffee shed,' said the kanakapillai.

'Let her fits cease,' said Muthamma. She had laid Sivakami on her lap and was wiping her face with the edge of her sari.

As the convulsions subsided, they carried her to the coffee shed. They could not carry her to her hut, for it was more than two miles away and they would have had to carry her through a difficult terrain. Instead, they laid her in the damp and filthy coffee shed and in a short while she started having her labour pains.

'Muthamma, you too are pregnant. This woman has epileptic fits, you should not be staying here, it's not good for you,' said a woman in the crowd, echoing a belief prevalent among them.

'It's alright. The same thing could happen to me, then what would I do without you people?' said Muthamma, as she firmly held on to Sivakami's hands and feet.

'Can one of you go get hot water brewed with some crushed dried ginger?' asked Muthamma.

They sent word to Sivakami's husband Ramasamy, and he arrived as soon as he could.

Racked by pain the entire morning, Sivakami gave birth to a boy that afternoon. The infant that had ripped its way out of her body was a freak child. It was not like the other children born on the estate. The baby was as fair and soft as the white mist, with soft brown hair, and ash grey eyes. All of them stared at this child, wonderstruck. Getting over their initial shock, they started whispering among themselves. The news of this strange baby spread through the estate and quickly reached even the men working in the fields. Sivakami's husband understood the situation on seeing the baby. He requested the kangany to make immediate arrangements to transfer Sivakami to their layyam.

'Have you heard the news?' Muthamma asked her husband Velan, later that evening.

'What is it?' asked Velan, his thoughts elsewhere.

'Our Sivakami has had a baby, round and pink, like a watermelon. But she is not too well, she had fits this morning.'

'Yes, I heard about it. What is it to you, why are dancing attendance like she is some long lost relative or something?' asked Velan, irritated with her.

'Whoever she is, she was the first to help us when we were new to this place. Tomorrow the same thing could easily happen to me, then who would care for me?' said Muthamma, feeling sorry for Sivakami.

'What is there to be sorry about? The dorai is there to give her what she wants. The kangany is also there to see to her needs. You are a fool if you think she needs you,' said Velan.

'You should have seen the baby. He's so beautiful, people will cast an evil eye on him,' said Muthamma.

'Enough of this talk. Mind your own business and don't poke your nose into all this. Otherwise I will get really mad,' warned Velan as he walked out.

12

When Velan received word from his first wife again, he approached the kangany reluctantly for a loan.

'Ayya, show some mercy and please give me some money,' pleaded Velan.

'You are becoming a pest, always asking for money. You think money grows on trees? You want an advance to buy food, you want a loan to buy clothes, you seem to need to borrow for everything!' the kangany rebuked him.

'I ask you because it's time I went home to my village, to see my first wife and children.'

'Get away from here! As it is you owe us money, as if that's not enough, now you want a loan to go to India?! Go away! Stop hounding me for more money, pay all your debts and then you can go to hell for all I care.'

'What, have you come once again asking for money?' taunted the kanakapillai, entering the fray.

'Ayya, if you could just give me something to meet my expenses...' said Velan, approaching the kanakapillai.

'Wait, let me check your account, and see what's possible. Hmm...it's just the two of you working on the plantation isn't it?' said the kanakapillai, as he checked him out with the corner of his eyes. Velan pretended not to notice this. He took the large ledger, turned the pages, pretended to check something out and said, 'Alright, come again this evening, after you finish work. We'll see what can be done,' said the kanakapillai dismissively. Just then the sinna dorai came in. Seeing that Velan and Ramasamy were the only ones hanging around, he wanted to know why they were not in the field.

Unable to offer a good explanation, Velan left the place, feeling dejected.

As her pregnancy progressed, Muthamma found it difficult to walk up and down the mountain terrain. Her cough also got worse. One day, unable to continue any further, she sat down by the coffee bushes, trying to get her breath back. That day she did not report to work.

'Atha, aren't you feeling too good?' Valli asked her mother. It was very evident from her mother's face that she was seriously ill. Muthamma quietly leaned against the wall, and in a little while she started having her labour pains and soon delivered a baby girl.

When Velan returned from work, Suppan gave him the news.

'Valli, hey Valli!' Velan called out to his daughter, as he walked in.

'She has gone to fetch water,' Muthamma mumbled from inside the layyam.

'Suppa, ask Mookan to buy some tobacco for me. Also bring my pruning knife which I have left with Kakkan,' said Velan, as he washed his muddied feet before entering the room.

'Muthamma, is the child alright?' He asked from the doorway.

'It's fine,' said Muthamma, in a disgruntled voice.

'Don't worry, you'll be fine. Nothing happens according to our plans. It is all the will of god,' Velan said as he took a look at the child.

'Ayya, I have left some coffee for you near the stove, have it while it's hot. I have to go back for more water,' said Valli, as she left the layyam.

'Vela, is it true Muthamma has had the child?' Mookan asked as he came in. 'Here is the tobacco you had asked for. The dorai told us that we have to plant the seedlings before the rains, otherwise it would rot. That's why it took us so long today. We were working in the lower forests today, and my god, you should have seen the number of snakes slithering all over the place—there must have been hundreds of them. We are lucky to be alive! The dorai asked us to light a fire, that's only going to drive them all to the upper slopes. As it is Kakkan tells me there are hundreds of snakes crawling around their shacks.'

'We also planted tea seedlings between the coffee bushes today. Did you see the coffee plants? They are all shrivelling and the leaves are infected. The periya dorai and sinna dorai were talking about it,' said Velan.

'That's true. Why don't you talk to the dorai and get a job for Suppan?' asked Mookan.

I have been thinking about it, but I don't want him to be harassed the way we are. I want to send my son's back to our village,' said Velan.

' That is a good plan. But then, why don't you let him work in the estate for as long as he is here.'

'Once you get caught in this life there is no escaping it. These fellows are like leeches, they will let you go only after sucking you dry,' said Velan with bitterness.

'You're right. Did you hear about this new fellow Karuppan, he tried to run away yesterday. He escaped to the village, where he was caught and brought over. They tied up his limbs and he was beaten till he became unconscious. People say he may not survive the night. Poor thing...a young fellow. He did not know what he was getting into,' said Mookan.

'They will do the same thing to our boy too, if we send him to work. Let's see, but I must do something about this hand-to-mouth existence. We cannot go on like this. Muthamma will need at least another month before she can return to work, besides her cough is also taking its toll on her.'

'Think before you decide on anything,' advised Mookan. Muthamma's coughing kept punctuating their talk.

This new idea festered in Velan's mind for some days. Meanwhile another message from Sellatha helped him arrive at a decision. He went straight to the sinna dorai in the presence of the kangany.

'Ayya, please give my son Suppan some work here, I wish to go to my village for a while,' said Velan.

The kangany explained Velan's request to the sinna dorai.

'I'll think about it. I'll let you know tomorrow when you report at the roll-call shed,' said the sinna dorai.

The kangany was mad at Velan. As soon as the dorai left, he took him to task.

'How dare you bring this up before the dorai! You have become that bold, have you?' He growled.

'No ayya, I came here to ask you, it just happened that the dorai too was here,' explained Velan. He knew there was no point antogonising the kangany.

'If you need anything you better come to me, understand? Don't ever try this again?' threatened the kangany.

That evening he told Mookan what had happened.

'The sinna dorai looks like a good man. It's this kangany and kanakapillai who have made the periya dorai what he is—depraved,' said Mookan.

The next day, the sinna dorai gave Velan permission to go to India. He also told him that he would employ Suppan. The moment Velan heard this, he was relieved. The thought of going back to his village gave Velan a new lease of life, he was excited. 'Muthamma! Valli! I am going to India!' he rushed home that evening and announced to his wife and daughter.

'Are you really going to India? Is it true?' asked Valli, surprised.

'I wonder how our village is?' mused Muthamma. These days she could hardly speak without being overcome by a bout of coughing. She tried the medicines given at the dispensary, and several home-made herbal concoctions, but to no avail. In spite of her frail health she had to nurse the baby. The starved child constantly cried for want of nourishment from her mother's dried up breasts.

'How am I going to manage alone without you?' Muthamma asked.

'Mookan is here, so is Suppan. It's not as if I can take you with me, when you are so sick. Even if I can, will these fellows let me?'

'You are right. Bound to this place, there is no way out for us,' said Muthamma dejected.

'Atha, here, get up and have this kanji,' said Valli

Velan suddenly realised that much of the household chores were now borne by Valli. 'How much work will this little girl have to do on her own?'

'I'll manage, appu. Will you bring bangles for me?' asked Valli, excited by the prospect.

'What? Bangles?' laughed Velan, 'The child has grown into a young girl....and an intelligent one at that...' he laughed again showing his betel-stained teeth.

'Of course, she's grown. Do you think she is still a child?' said Mookan, as he walked in, listening to the conversation.

'Valli, get me some hot water, will you?' he requested.

'I am going to our village, Mooka!' Velan told him excitedly.

'So, the dorai has given you permission?'

'I asked the kangany in the presence of the sinna dorai.'

'You know how these fellows are otherwise, they will always give you some excuse. I also asked him to give Suppan a job. Let him work till I return from Senthur. We'll see after that,' said Velan.

'Oh my god! Oh my....' Muthamma groaned out loud. Her emaciated body looked grotesque in the lamplight.

'Did Sivakami come here?' asked Mookan, softly.

'She did, but she dreads meeting any of you,' said Muthamma.

'Her child is fine, only thing is he has shinning grey eyes like a cat,' said Valli.

'Why talk about all that? It is not for us, lowly folks,' Velan replied.

'Yesterday there was a fight, I think, with the kangany. They were talking about something and suddenly it became a loud brawl. He left in a huff,' said Valli.

'Was it yesterday? When was that?' asked Mookan interestedly.

'He came after you had all left for work,' said Valli.

'He is capable of anything, being a big shot and everything,' said Mookan.

Velan was completely engrossed with his oncoming journey to India. At the end of the month he was to go to his village with some others and a kangany from a neighbouring estate.

One evening, Velan was late returning home, as he had to visit the store to buy grocery. The moon's silvery rays lit the night. The play of light and shadow, among the coffee bushes, made the night beautiful and eerie. Velan conceded that such lush beauty cannot be seen in his village, but his heart still ached for his country. He once again longed to walk on the ridges running around the fields, get his feet muddied ploughing with his bullocks, and, have a refreshing bath in the village pond. Velan was shaken out of these thoughts, on hearing voices in the dark.

'Sivakami, don't go to that kangany fellow. For how long are you going to put up with your lame husband? Just say one word and I'll...'

Velan thought the voice sounded like it was Mookan. He stood rooted to the spot in shock and surprise.

'What can I do? That kangany fellow is harassing me, he says he will kill me. The periya dorai is afraid, now that the sinna dorai is here. He is now bothering me to come along with him to the bungalow. My husband is only interested in the money, he does not care how he gets it,' said Sivakami, her voice laced with sadness and despair.

Velan felt wretched hearing these words.

He wondered at what was right and what was wrong. He could not understand these things anymore. He had never dreamt there could be anything between Mookan and Sivakami. He was really surprised at how this could have happened and wondered how this was going to end. Not wanting to be caught overhearing, he quickly walked towards his layyam.

13

Two or three weeks after Velan's departure to India, Hamilton Estate was visited by the deadly smallpox disease. It spread like wild fire, claiming the lives of more than a hundred workers. Velan's children, Valli and Rengan, were also afflicted. Valli survived, but Rengan succumbed to the epidemic. They buried Rengan under the tea bushes.

Muthamma was overwhelmed by this tragedy. She cursed the gods who put her through such a trial, that too when Velan was away. She wondered how she could possibly explain this to Velan.

'Atha, don't cry, we are all there for you. I will explain to appu when he comes,' Valli comforted her.

By the time Velan returned to Ceylon the monsoon had set in—the howling winds, the chilly fog, the slushy ground and the proliferating leeches, made their lives miserable.

On the day of Velan's arrival, the sun had put out a few anaemic rays that reflected grandly on the stagnant puddles of water. Velan approached the plantation with loathing. As soon as he set foot on that wet soil his mind flew to his village. Trusting the kangany, had been a big mistake—he was now stuck with one family in India and another in Ceylon. Trying to run two households was like holding on to a piece of log that has been lit on both sides. He felt rage and anger overwhelm him. He had seen Sellatha's plight in India, and here, he was aware of Muthamma's miseries—he felt devastated by the futility of their lives.

The watchman opened the massive iron gates and let him in. Hearing the gate shut firmly behind him, Velan once again felt like a prisoner. Against his will an unknown fear took hold of him.

'Appu, is that you? You've come back?' cried Valli excitedly, rushing to her father.

Velan, buried in his thoughts, was surprised to see Valli. Since he had walked all the way from the port to reach Hamilton Estate, his clothes were dirty and his hair was matted with dust. He smiled, flashing his betel-stained teeth, but his daughter's eyes were bleak and could not return his smile. Tears welled up, choking the words he wished to speak.

'Valli, Valli my child!' He held her and wept aloud, on hearing that Rengan had lost his life to small pox.

After their weeping subsided and a calm descended on them, Velan raised his head and looked at Valli. He saw that she had become lean and frail, all skin and bones. He felt a sharp pain tug at his heart; he hugged her close, protectively.

'Come appu, have some hot coffee. The baby will start crying, let's go home,' said Valli, as she led him to their layyam.

'How is Muniamma?' Velan asked, wanting to know about the baby he had left behind.

'She is fine. Have you brought bangles for me? How is periatha?' Valli kept asking him about their village, as they walked homewards.

Valli gave the news of Velan's arrival to her mother, when she went to give her lunch. She carried Muniamma with her. Ever since Rengan's death, the baby could not be left behind at home. Sometimes Muthamma had to carry the baby to the field, she had no time to return to their layyam to nurse the child. She would then tie a cradle on a tree with an old sari and put the child to sleep, while she worked.

That evening, sounds of gossip, interspersed with loud lamentations, could be heard from Velan's room in the layyam. People dropped in to find out the news from their village. Velan was also updated on the news of the estate.

'What, Sivakami's husband Ramasamy has also died?' asked Velan, astonished.

'Yes, poor thing, she is suffering a lot,' said Muthamma.

'It's probably for the best,' thought Velan, looking at Mookan with a sidelong glance.

'The fellow died leaving her alone, with a baby to look after.'

'You're talking as if it's his child. It's all her fate...' said Velan. All through this conversation Mookan looked out, pretending disinterest.

'The kangany does not pay her much attention these days. With the sinna dorai here, the periya dorai too seems to have quietened down,' said Muthamma.

Velan was still keenly observing Mookan. He saw that his eyes had filled with tears.

'Valli,' he called out to his daughter, 'Come here, child. Kali's son asked about you. Chittu also wanted to know how you are. Kali sent this piece of cloth for you.' He sucessfully steered the conversation that was proving to be painful to Mookan.

Months sped past. The workers braved the slushy, wet slopes and the gusty winds of the rainy season, armed with only a thin blanket. Velan meanwhile was plunged in depression.

He always believed he would have two sons who would be his support in these alien shores. Rengan's death was a huge blow to him.

Muthamma walked around like a madwoman. She would mechanically go about doing her work, talking to herself, muttering under her breath. Ever since Rengan's death, she seemed disturbed—the constant lamentation had numbed her soul.

As the years passed in this manner, Velan's family got habituated to its many trials and tribulations.

'Muthamma, why doesn't Sivakami marry again?' asked Velan, one day.

'I don't know, I wonder why she's like that? She is just exposing herself to all kinds of talk,' said Muthamma.

'Why shouldn't our Mookan marry her? Everyone knows about their relationship, it would be better if they got married,' said Velan.

'She is the one refusing him, at least that's what people say. Besides he has a wife in India,' said Muthamma.

'As though he's ever going to go back to the village to live with his wife? You are a fool!' said Velan.

'Vela, Vela!' the excited voice of Mookan rang through the layyam. Velan got up and went outside. 'Vela, did you hear the news? Our sinna dorai's horse slipped and fell, throwing him off its back!'

'Oh god, why should this happen to our sinna dorai. Nothing ever happens to those good-for-nothing crooks!' said Velan, as he and Mookan hurried towards the office.

'I saw men carrying him to the bungalow. I wonder if he is badly hurt.'

'Good thing he did not hit his head on the rock,' said Velan.

'It looks like he hit a tree,' said Mookan.

They went up to the office and not knowing what to do, they waited outside. They gathered that the sinna dorai had hurt his head and broken his leg. After hanging around for some more time, they returned to their homes.

Two days later, they were told that his condition had worsened and that he had been removed to a hospital in Kandy. It took four to five months for him to recover. During his absence the administration of the estate ran amok, with the kangany and kanakapillai ruling the place with arrogance and ruthlessness. The periya dorai began to drink heavily and he staggered around like an animal in heat. Because of this, there was no end to the atrocities committed by the kangany and kanakapillai.

One day, they had heavy rains, the winds too conspired to rip the roofs off their homes, lightning and thunder made it impossible for them to sleep. The storm continued all night. The rain water ran like a river, rushing down the slope, and the mud and slush made it impossible for them to step out. Velan, huddled up in a blanket, sat by the kitchen fire, trying to warm himself. Muthamma would drift to sleep, only to be awakened by the rolling thunder. Mookan slept by the doorway.

It was almost dawn when Velan found himself finally drifting to sleep. The rain had subsided, leaving behind an eerie stillness. A faint moon lent its rays to the sky. Suddenly, on hearing an angry exchange of voices, Velan woke up with a start.

'Take your hands off me, or I'll shout,' he heard Sivakami's distressed voice, raised in anger.

'You have got together with that fellow, Mookan, and are not heeding us anymore. Do you know who I am? I can get rid of him for good!' threatened a male voice. It was the kangany's voice.

'Has he become greater than the dorai? You ass, you know you can live like a queen. You better come with me if you know what is good for you,' the kangany bullied Sivakami.

'Thoo,' she spat at him. 'Have you no shame? I said I do not wish to come, you better get away from here! I have seen your dorai and the likes of him. I work, and you pay me for my work. You are not giving anything for free are you?'

'Do you know who I am? You whore! Have you become that impertinent? Wait and see what I am going to do to you and that fellow,' he bellowed angrily.

'Do what you can, there is nothing you haven't already done. Get out,' Sivakami screamed at him.

It sounded like he was trying to drag her by force and she was resisting the attempt. Velan saw Mookan rush to Sivakami's aid. He caught hold of the kangany by his collar, forcing him to let go of Sivakami.

'What are you doing here? Is she your wife? Get out!' the kangany ordered. Mookan would not budge.

'Yes, she is my wife!' claimed Mookan, maddened by the situation.

'Chi, you dog! He has no way of earning a living, but look at his big mouth? Just you wait, I will get even with both of you!' said the kangany menacingly, as he left the place.

'Now that the sinna dorai is not here, you will definitely be up to your old tricks. Go on, do what you can,' challenged Mookan. The words were blown away in the wind, as the kangany walked down the hillside.

Velan, who was watching all this from his dwelling, hid himself when he saw the kangany leave. He wondered where all this was going to lead them.

His speculation was not wrong. By the end of that month, Mookan went to the office to look at the accounts concerning his wages.

'Oh, is that you Mooka? You have come to ask about your wages, have you?' asked the kangany, haughtily.

'They are refusing to give me groceries in the store saying I have to pay all my debts before I buy any more. How do I eat, ayya?' asked Mookan, boldly.

'Oh, you have come to look into your accounts, have you? Kanakapillai, will you look into his accounts?' said the kangany.

The kanakapillai flipped a few pages of the ledger and whispered something into the kangany's ears.

'You have so much debt in your account and you want more money? I cannot give you anymore. You work this month and we will see what can be done,' said the kangany.

'But how do I feed myself?' Mookan asked him angrily.

'What do I care? It is not my business,' said the kangany, dismissively.

'Ayya, do you expect me to work for you, while I am starving?'

'Yes, I only want my work completed,' said the kangany cruelly, turning away from him.

'I am asking you about my accounts, and you are just walking away callously. Tell me what are all these debts that you keep talking about? Are you trying to cheat us?' asked Mookan, outraged.

'What did you say? You dare talk back to me? Do you think this is my only job, looking at your accounts?! You cur, how cocky and insolent you have become!' yelled the kangany.

'Don't we look like human beings to you? Are we animals or what? You people do nothing, but still you stuff yourself with food. Here we are, hard at work and even denied food to eat,' Mookan burst out angrily.

His reply infuriated the kangany and the kanakapillai.

'Tie this fellow to a tree, the scoundrel,' they ordered. The watchman caught Mookan and strapped him to a tree. The kangany went inside and said something to the periya dorai. The periya dorai immediately came out and asked for his whip. He was completely drunk and did not know what he was doing. He whipped Mookan mercilessly, ignoring his screams, until he dropped unconscious.

The kangany was not satisfied. He further inflamed the dorai, who now glared at him like a menacing wolf. He looked at him like he would like to tear him to pieces and make a meal out of him.

The dorai called out to the clerk. A meek and submissive figure, rushed out and stood deferentially.

'Take this fellow to the police station. Tell them he is a troublemaker and give this note to the magistrate, go.' He wrote a short note and handed it to the clerk.

Mookan did not understand why he was being sent to jail. 'Sami, I will not talk like this again. Sami, please let me go! Please!' he pleaded, but it fell on deaf ears.

They chained him and dragged him to the police station, where without a hearing he was sentenced to six months imprisonment.

This incident decimated Velan's belief in life and people. Even the little hopes he had nurtured, crumbled completely, leaving him lost and numb.

14

The tea saplings that had been planted by the labourers, were now mature bushes, ready for picking. Those who had come to the garden as small girls, were now young women, in the flush of youth. Valli too was one among them.

'Vela, don't you think it's time you got Valli married?' the kangany asked with concern.

'You are right, ayya, I too am on the look out for a good boy. They say there is a boy, belonging to our caste, in Rasikollai Rasa Estate. If the boy is good, we have to do something about Valli's marriage,' replied Velan.

'Yes, we have to be careful in these matters. Why don't you find someone from our estate and get her married?'

'No, ayya, there is a relative of my wife's, an aunt's son, we are considering him.'

'Whatever you decide, see that the boy is not located too far. If you wish, you can bring him to our estate, I'll find a job for him. It will be difficult for you, if she lives too far away,' said the kangany. He made it sound as though he was genuinely interested in Velan's welfare, when in truth he was only looking to recruit a new hand, free of cost.

Suddenly, realising that his sidekick was missing, the kangany called out, 'Hey boy, where did you go? Go and get me some snuff,' he ordered. He then enquired about Sivakami.

'She is still not alright, the swelling is still present,' said Muthamma.

'Is the child better now?'

'A little better...'

'I see,' said the kangany, as he walked away twirling his umbrella.

'Oh my, my! What pride, what arrogance...' remarked Suppan, snidely.

'Keep quiet! Don't let your mouth get you into trouble,' Velan admonished his son.

'Why this sudden interest, I wonder. He must have something up his sleeve,' said Suppan. Just then Mookan returned from the river after his bath. He had completed his term at the prison and was now a broken man.

'Mama, that great man tells us we have to get our Valli married,' Suppan briefed Mookan.

'I saw the kangany going down the hillside. Vela, before something untoward happens, it is better to get Valli married,' said Mookan as he dried his hair.

'Yes, it would be difficult to guard our daughter amongst these wolves,' said Muthamma.

'Fine, let's look for an auspicious day, take the kangany's permission, and go see this boy. We will help him settle in our estate,' decided Velan.

Valli blushed listening to this conversation.

'What is this? Are you already feeling shy?' asked Muthamma.

'She is no longer a child, naturally she feels shy,' said Sivakami, who was listening to the talk about Valli's marriage. Her swollen legs hampered her movement as she tried to walk to Muthamma's room.

Now that the talk of Valli's marriage came up, all the neighbours joined in.

ଓ

That same month, Mookan and Kakkan went to Rasikollai Rasa Estate to see the boy. They asked Kuppan, the boy's father if he was willing to get his son Sengamalai married to Valli. He accepted the proposal.

'Let me come and see the girl once, we can discuss the other details later,' said Kuppan.

Kuppan's son Sengamalai was a tall and handsome young man, with a fine moustache, thick dark hair, and rippling muscles.

'How many children have you?' asked Mookan.

'Well, it is more than ten years since I came here and god has blessed me with ten children,' said Kuppan

'How do you manage with ten children?'

'What can I do, I have to manage somehow. Only Sengamalai and Kayambu are working. The others are still too young,' said Kuppan.

'Alright, let us look for an auspicious day and get them married. Come and see Valli. She is really a very pretty girl. Besides, she is a wonderful person,' said Kakkan. Mookan and Kakkan, having carried out their assignment, returned to Hamilton Estate.

Forests had surrounded these hills, when they had first come to Ceylon. Now they were transformed into well-laid out tea plantations. Looking at it from distance, one saw tea bushes stretching in all directions like a green carpet. The red dirt road on one side and the cascading waterfall on the other, adorned these sweeping hills.

The heady eucalyptus trees and coffee plants, further spread a warm fragrance around Hamilton Estate.

'So Mooka, how did the talks go?' asked Velan, when he found Mookan and Kakkan waiting at his doorstep when he returned from work.

'The boy looks good, but the family is too big. Nevertheless, I liked the boy,' said Mookan.

'He looks like a mischievous rogue, a good match for Valli,' Kakkan said, in a teasing tone, when he caught sight of Valli.

'Why mama, what do you suppose is wrong with me?' Valli rose to the teasing bait.

'Don't you know you are a great prattler? Let that boy come, I'll tell him how to handle you. Vela, you better make the arrangements soon, this girl is becoming too cheeky,' said Kakkan, enjoying himself.

'Do I look like a fool to you? I don't want marriage or any such thing,' said Valli, as she blushed prettily.

'Why my princess, do you think your father is going to feed you forever?' asked Kakkan.

'If not me, then who else is going to look after my daughter? No man is worthy of my daughter—he wouldn't even compare to the dust under her feet,' Velan replied, puffing with pride.

'Alright, alright! I am going to the river. Father and daughter can do what they want,' said Mookan, as he walked away.

'Have some coffee before you go. Valli, bring some coffee for us child,' said Velan.

The groom's family came over to Hamilton Estate to finalise the marriage. Velan had invited the kangany and the kanakapillai for the proceedings. Velan sent word for them as soon as the groom's party arrived.

'Vela, are these the groom's people?' enquired the kangany as he arrogantly appraised them. 'Hmm, the boy seems fine, do what is necessary. Remember, you have no one but Suppan here for you. Get this boy to stay with you on the estate. Anyway, it's time we got going. I have some work in the upper slopes, and the dorai too wanted to have a word with me. I'll come at leisure,' said the kangany, as he prepared to leave with the kanakapillai.

'Let Valli come and live with us for some time, later we will see about their coming here,' said Kuppan, the groom's father.

'Shall we have the wedding next month?' asked Mookan.

'Actually we can think of having it a little later,' said Muthamma, who knew her life would become more arduous without Valli.

Valli, sitting near the cooking fire, was quietly stealing glances at Sengamalai, the groom. He too was similarly engaged, each looking away when their eyes met. As the elders held their talks, these two were blissfully transported to a different world.

Now that Valli was engaged to be married, the girls on the plantation teased her constantly.

'Valli, how is the groom?' asked one.

'Don't say groom, say "machan",' said another, and they all burst out laughing.

'Stop it, will you!' Valli pleaded with them.

'Are you feeling shy? It all comes with being engaged...'

'Please, stop teasing for some time,' implored Valli.

'Valli, stop pretending to be so naive.'

'Do you know what he would do to you...'

'Oh! She knows alright. She looks like a small girl, but she might actually teach us a few tricks.'

Just then, the kanakapillai came along and ordered them to get back to work, 'What is all this laughing and chatter? Get to work, all of you.'

Something unfortunate happened before Valli's marriage.

Sivakami's swollen legs got better and she resumed work. Mookan and Sivakami were still involved with each other.

One day the kangany accosted him in the workfield saying, 'Hey Mooka! Come here.' Taking him aside he said, 'Mooka, I am telling this for your own good. Leave Sivakami alone, otherwise you are asking for trouble.'

Mookan was infuriated.

'I am going to marry Sivakami, do you understand! You keep your hands off her!' Mookan answered defiantly.

'You rascal, you dare wag your tail at me, I will just cut it short. Be careful! If you do as I say you will survive, if not, do you know what I will do to you and your arrogance?'

'I have seen what you can do! Go ahead, do what you want!' Mookan challenged him.

The kangany's fury rose beyond control. 'You dare talk back to me? Even the dorai does not speak to me in this manner. You are an insignificant fellow, who was brought here yesterday, and you dare thwart me?' raged the kangany. He hit Mookan forcefully with his umbrella. Before Mookan could get over the shock, he hit him again. Mookan was standing by the mountain path, close to a precipice. The ground under him gave way and he fell off the edge, rolling down the valley. There were no trees to stay his fall.

'Aiyo,' he screamed, as he rolled down the ravine.

The other workers in the place rescued him. By the time they got him to his layyam, he had lost consciousness. His skull had split open and he was bleeding profusely. He died without regaining consciousness.

'Aiyo, Mooka!' Velan cried out in agony. 'You have left me orphaned!'

Sivakami was inconsolable, 'Oh, they have killed you! You were killed because of me, this sinner! Let god take your murderer to the worst hell! Let him be destroyed,' she lamented. Muthamma tried to console her, but to no avail.

Kakkan and Suppan dug a grave under a tea bush, not too far from Rengan's grave. The labourers gathered around and buried him.

They could not ask why this happened or how it happened. No one dared question this mishap.

Valli's marriage was postponed by a month.

Velan was very dejected 'The man who arranged this marriage is gone! Who is my support now?' he lamented aloud.

Valli too deeply felt the loss of her Mookan mama.

15

'Valli, don't forget me once your machan comes along,' Kakkan would tease her.

'Oh, stop teasing me mama,' Valli would say, as she walked towards the river to fetch water.

'Valli, Valli! Listen to this,' he would say and start belting out a folk-song.

Did you hear, my dears
She says she wants not to be teased
But the machan she's been waiting for
Does not have a coin in his pocket.

Oh you proud beauty
Walking all lovelorn
My little cousin Valli
Is waiting for her machan

He came crossing the seas
He came braving the forests
He came running to her
Searching all Kandy, for his bride.

Fine whiskered is he
Ariya Kollai Kuppan's son
Looking for his teasing love,
He came searching
Sengamalai.

This song reverberated across the hills. Valli, who was on her way to fetch water, laughed all the way to the river. People listening to this ditty were amused by it.

'The song is very nice,' said Velan.

'Not bad! Our Kakkan machan can really sing,' said one woman.

'Of course, my girls, I can sing, I can dance, will you join me?' he asked the the girls, who were hurrying down the slopes.

'Looks like Kakkan machan has found his youth once again! Is it time for Valli's marriage, or this old man's?' teased a young girl.

'Hey, hey, you brat, wait. Are you calling me old?' he stood up, challenging them. The women ran down the slopes laughing at him.

The day of the marriage arrived. Everyone on the estate arrived that evening to attend the ceremony. The women sat around, chewing betel, gossiping, teasing one another.

The ceremony was being held in the evening for the convenience of all the workers on the estate. There was no priest to officiate the ceremony.

Velan dutifully invited the kangany and kanakapillai. He told the kangany, 'Ayya, you are our elder. Please do preside over the wedding.' He also formally invited both the periya dorai and sinna dorai, offering them betel leaves with his invitation, as was the custom.

As his contribution, the kangany gave a small loan to Velan, and bought a sari and blouse for Valli from Kandy. He, of course, promptly noted down these expenses in Velan's account.

That morning, the bridegroom's people had arrived with betel leaves, coconut, fruits and other paraphernalia. They had gathered at Velan's layyam, and also made use of his neighbour Sivakami's room.

Valli sat in a secluded corner. She had attained puberty only a few months ago. She only knew what their poverty-ridden life had taught her. She was not worldlywise, and she was now awestruck and apprehensive about what was happening to her. Dressed in the inexpensive sari and blouse given by the kangany, her childish figure appeared doubled in size. Her hair was neatly combed and braided. Her face was radiant by the light of the tin lamp and the brass kuthuvilakku.

The groom, Sengamalai, could not have been very old, probably no more than eighteen. With his hair neatly in place, a high forehead, betel-stained teeth, and a sprouting moustache he looked grand.

'Sengamalai, how are you? So, do you like your girl?' asked Kakkan. Sengamalai was at a loss for words.

'The girl is very sharp, she can give you a hard time!' said someone in the crowd.

'She cannot play games with our Sengamalai, he is a tough one, you know,' defended someone from Sengamalai's family.

'We will know with time, who gets the better of whom. They look like they are made for each other.'

'Come on, everyone! Bring the groom, it's time,' someone announced from Velan's room.

By the faint light of the kuthuvilakku, Valli was married to Sengamalai. Velan asked the kangany to bless the couple.

'Alright, the boy does look like a good sort,' said the kangany. He told the groom, 'Why don't you settle down here. You will be a big help to Velan.'

'May you be blessed with sixteen children and a long life,' offered the kanakapillai, for his part.

'Our girl Valli is a good worker,' said the kangany, for the benefit of the groom's family.

The new moon shed its faint rays which filtered through the trees. Thousands of stars had blossomed, adorning the sky.

Those seated outside the layyam rose, as the kangany and kanakapillai came out.

The kangany looked smart and dapper in his smart silk vetti, gold embroidered shawl, long coat and majestic turban.

He reminded them of the king who appeared in the tales of Pulithevan. Kakkan smiled to himself and started singing a ditty.

Machan went to Kandy
sold his earstuds for a meal
Machan who went to Colombo
Where is the money you had earned?

Six months in Kandy
three months on the ship
All my money from Colombo
I have spent it on the way.

Look at the wastrel groom
standing like a pillar of wood
Sprouting moustache on his face
tell me dear, is he a worthy man?

He came looking for his love
with not a paise in his pocket
He came looking for his Valli
with not a paise to his name.

'Kakkan sings well,' said some in the crowd.

In this manner, the festivities continued through the night. The day after the wedding, Valli, Sengamalai and his parents left for Rasikollai Rasa Estate. This was the first time Valli was stepping out of Hamilton Estate, ever since her arrival all those years ago.

Valli was apprehensive about her new life. She was leaving her father's home to live with relative strangers. She felt as if she was being pushed into an abyss.

'You go along with her and stay for a day,' Muthamma instructed Velan.

'I wonder what the kangany will say?'

'What can he say? She is very young, how will she manage? She knows no one there.'

'Alright, I will ask Kakkan to accompany me,' said Velan. He suddenly felt the loss of Mookan, who had always treated Valli as his own child. Grief choked him.

The thought of Valli leaving, made Muthamma feel as though an essential part of herself was being ripped apart. She now felt that they should have found a boy for her in Hamilton Estate itself. But it was too late for regrets. Besides, there was no boy, suitable for her daughter in the estate. She knew how risky it was to take care of a young, unmarried girl under such circumstances. She consoled herself thinking that she would have anyway had to part with Valli even if they had gotten her married to someone from Senthur.

Valli was still a child at heart. Everything seemed strange and new to her. She had seen many weddings back home at Senthur. But when it came to her own, it was different. She still could not believe she was now a married woman. The thought of beginning her new life with a strange man and an unknown family was something beyond her comprehension. She did not anticipate a life filled with trials and tribulations. But the thought of venturing on a new life with strangers made her anxious and confused.

'It is getting late, shall we go?' asked Kuppan, Sengamalai's father.

'Yes, we are ready,' replied Kakkan, who could see that Velan was visibly shaken.

'Atha, atha,' cried out Valli, overwhelmed by the idea of separation. She held on to her mother, crying inconsolably. Her distress moved her friends and family to tears.

'Come on now. You are just going to the neighbouring estate. We'll see you often,' said Sivakami, trying to console her.

They started on their journey, Valli carrying her belongings with her. She was to start this new life with three sets of petticoats and blouses, one sari, a water pot and a comb. Her neighbours had all left for work, so there was no crowd to see her off.

Valli, with her head bowed, followed her mother-in-law Ponnamma. As a child she would hold on to her father's hand and walk by his side. She knew she could not do that any more. Valli's mother-in-law, Ponnamma, did not offer a comforting word or gesture to the weeping Valli.

Kakkan noticing Valli's distress tried to lighten the situation with his ready humour.

'Vela, shall we go to the toddy shop on our way home?' asked Kakkan.

'It's been a long time,' said Velan.

'Let's go now,' insisted Kuppan, Sengamalai's father,

They decided to visit the toddy tavern right away. They walked through a narrow path to reach the toddy tavern in the outskirts of a village. Having had their fill they walked to Rasikollai Rasa Estate, feeling light-headed and joyous. Valli, Sengamalai and Ponnamma did not partake the liquor. The rest of them were now staggering under its influence. The ever buoyant Kakkan broke into a song.

They reached Valli's new home in a pleasant haze.

16

Valli began her new life at Rasikollai Rasa Estate as Sengamalai's young wife. Sengamalai was as inexperienced as Valli, without any knowledge of the outside world.

Valli's father-in-law Kuppan looked like a thug. His thick unkempt hair, blood-shot eyes, hollow cheeks, stained teeth and protruding bones made him look gaunt and severe. Valli was terrified of him.

Sengamalai's mother, Ponnamma, was no better than her husband. She was a strong and able-bodied woman with a voice that grated on your nerves. Her disdainful attitude quashed

Valli's spirit. Valli had seen her stepmother Sellatha behave in such a coarse manner, but she had not lived with her for long. Valli was used to her father Velan's genial temperament and her mother's patient understanding. This new life was totally alien to her. The life with her in-laws was filled with nasty bickerings and raucous fights. Valli could only stare in astonishment as she witnessed such scenes.

Rasikollai Rasa Estate was different in many ways from Hamilton Estate. It was much larger—one division filled with coffee, another with tea, interspersed with extensive forests spread across the mountain. You had to climb at least a thousand feet to reach the summit, and the estate itself spread across three thousand acres. Nawalapitiya was situated seven miles away and one could see small villages, with farmers cultivating paddy, on the other side. Valli's family lived on the eastern side of the plantation. That was the oldest part of the estate, and if one walked towards the north one saw a beautiful river coursing down the mountain. From the top of the mountain one could see the tea factory looking like a pigeon coop. The morning sun rose in all its glory, making the estate look ethereal. But with the setting sun, the play of shadows and eerie stillness made the place look haunted and frightening.

The plantation was run by the periya dorai, Edward Morrison and sinna dorai, Richard Maclean. Besides these, there were four periya kanganys, four sinna kanganys and four kanakapillais administering the four divisions of the estate. The division where Sengamalai and his parents worked, was overseen by the periya kangany, Sarattu Kandiah, the sinna kangany, Murukku Muthiah, and the kanakapillai, Veerappu Veeriah.

On the third day of her arrival at Rasikollai Rasa Estate, Valli was taken to the periya kangany and her name was registered for work.

Although the kangany was in need of workers for the estate, he affected a pose of considering the issue, cleared his throat and shook his head thoughtfully. Valli noted that he was tall and well-built like the dorai himself. He had combed his long, oiled hair and tied it into a knot. His dark complexion set off his few grey hairs, making them look like silver strands.

'Call the kanakapillai,' ordered the kangany.

'What is it ayya?' asked Veeriah meekly. Veeriah, who was haughty in general, displayed only diffidence to the kangany.

'Veeriah, see if you can register this girl. Kuppa, couldn't you find a better girl for your son? There are a few in our estate who would have been suitable,' said Kangany Kandhiah scornfully.

'Don't you know ayya, she is a relative of ours? We thought it would be good to keep her in the family.'

'Alright, alright. You better behave yourself girl. Now, what is your name?'

'Valli, ayya,' replied Kuppan, for his daughter-in-law.

'I will ask them to put her name on the rolls. Let us see if she is a good worker,' said Kangany Kandiah, as he walked away briskly. Valli's eyes fell upon the slippers he wore. She was totally fascinated by the sound they made. She was not used to Indians wearing footwear. Sengamalai stood beside her, stealing glances at his new wife.

'Ask her to begin work tomorrow. Let her learn to pick tea leaves and weed the grass in the fields. We will fix her pay later,' said the kanakapillai.

'Yes ayya,' said Kuppan.

'You go back to our layyam. Follow this path up the hillside. Take care,' said Sengamalai to his wife. Kuppan had already walked away without looking back.

Sengamalai was very young, and feared his parents greatly. Valli realised that he was not plucky like her brother Suppan. Sengamalai toed the line drawn by his parents, without a word of protest. But his parents lived a wayward life with no principles. They had six boys and three girls, the oldest among them was Sengamalai. Next came Maruthai, and the third was a girl, Kamakshi. The rest were very young. Kuppan, Ponnamma and Sengamalai were the only ones who went to work. Maruthai and Kamakshi took care of the children while they were at work. Maruthai was short and dark like his mother, Kamakshi, with her bones sticking out, took after her father.

Kamakshi was not at all pleased with the arrival of Valli. Valli, with her beautiful hair, lighter skin, round face and plump body, looked comely. Valli was made to sleep beside Kamakshi, ever since she stepped into her husband's home. She would cry herself to sleep every night, but there was no one to offer a word of comfort.

Valli began working in the estate soon. In the evenings she would be ordered around by her mother-in-law to fetch water, make tea and do the cooking.

'Cook some rice and make some curry to go with it.' 'Take the child and give her a bath.' She was expected to do many such chores.

Almost a month after her wedding, while she was returning from work, Sengamalai waylaid his wife, 'Valli, wait! Let me also come with you.'

'I am only going to our layyam,' said Valli, feeling very shy.

Even though they had been married for a month now, Sengamalai had hardly spoken a few words to her, especially when they were alone. Thus, when he made the attempt, she did not know how to react and stood there rooted to the spot.

'Valli, why don't you speak to me? Why won't you come near me?' he whispered softly.

She began to walk without offering a reply.

'Come, let us go to the river and then go home. I know all about your crying in the night. I too am awake in the night,' he told her.

'Valli, why are you not talking to me? If appu wasn't around, I would have surely come to you. Why do you cry when we are all there for you?' he slowly caught her hand.

She tried to pull away.

'I won't let you go, unless you promise to come to me tonight. Will you come?'

'Yes,' she said in a faint voice.

'Come let us wet our feet in the river before we return,' he said.

ꕥ

A gentle balmy wind, blew through the night. It was very quiet, and the stillness was broken only by the sound of snores and the howling jackals. Valli sat in a corner unable to sleep. There was no door to their room in the layyam, moonlight streamed in effortlessly.

'Valli, Valli,' whispered Sengamalai, calling out to his wife.

Valli looked up—surprise, fear, eagerness and wonder suffused her face. His love-lorn eyes pierced through her heart. A beautiful smile spread across his lips and eyes.

'Valli, come, will you?' he entreated, holding her hand gently.

Her heart filled with joy. She was assailed by a thousand thoughts. She knew he was about to lead her into a new world. Like a pigeon about to be caged, her heart hesitated to accept his invitation. At that instance, she was a tender bud—waiting to unfurl into a beautiful flower.

17

Valli and Sengamalai shared the single room, 10 feet by 12 feet, occupied by Kuppan, his wife and eight other children. This was hellish for Valli. The affection, care and attention that Sengamalai demonstrated at night was never on display during the day. He did exactly as his father and mother told him. This attitude irritated her.

Months passed by and Valli noticed that Kuppan went everywhere but to work. One day the sinna kangany asked Sengamalai, 'Why hasn't Kuppan come to work today?'

'I think he has a stomach ache,' replied Sengamalai.

'I know all about his stomach aches and his other aches. Let it be, I shall talk to the periya kangany about him and ask him to inquire into this. He has dug his own grave, there is nothing more to this,' said the sinna kangany as he walked away.

Sengamalai continued working, pretending not to have heard.

That evening, Sengamalai confronted his father who was in a drunken stupor, 'Ayya, the sinna kangany threatens to report to the periya kangany about you not coming to work,' he said.

'You keep going to the toddy tavern everyday, and you are going to get into trouble with the kangany,' said Ponnamma, as she walked in after work.

'Valli, did you fetch water? Come here, girl,' she shouted, venting her anger on her. Valli had just come back from work and was putting her basket away.

'What is it athai,' Valli asked.

'What are you doing? Can't you go early and fetch water? Have I got to tell you this everyday? When are you going to cook the rice?'

'I just came back from work. How can I do all this work? My legs are paining,' replied Valli.

'Your legs are paining?! I am sure they do. Oh my! Have you heard this story? So, do you expect *me* to fetch water and cook and serve you?' Ponnamma launched into a tirade.

'Why don't you ask Kamakshi to do it?' said Sengamalai.

'So you too have joined ranks with that wretch, have you? I can see she is a sly one, already bewitching my boy,' bellowed Ponnamma, as she dragged Valli by her hair and pushed her down.

'Go now, get on with your work. Kamakshi is not your personal maid,' said Ponnamma. People returning from work watched this scene as they passed by.

'Look at her, she dares talk back to me,' Ponnamma complained to them.

'She thinks she is a princess.' said Kuppan, joining the fray.

Valli, crying all the way, went with the water pot to fetch water. She sat there till it was dark and cried her heart out. The gurgling river drowned her sobs. The water was bitterly cold and the mist was getting denser. She took her water pot and started for home. She heard a rustle behind her in that deserted pathway. She turned and saw that it was the sinna dorai, Maclean, standing in the pathway.

Valli moved aside, to give him way.

'What are you doing here at this hour?' he asked. As he was very fair, she could see his face even in that darkening twilight. He stood tall and handsome, with his twinkling blue eyes and hair like spun gold.

'I came to fetch water,' she replied.

'In future you are not to come here at this time!' He strode away, having issued this order. Valli stood rooted to the spot, until she no longer heard his clicking boots.

Along with the other women in the estate, Valli went to work in the plantation and soon learnt the art of picking the tender leaves of the tea bushes. Days grew into months and Valli became pregnant.

One day it poured heavily. It was impossible to step out. Not many were going out to work that day. Valli, rather than put up with her mother-in-law's harassment, chose to cover herself with a blanket and go to work. She applied tobacco on her legs to keep the leeches away. She knew this would not be effective for long, for the rain would wash the tobacco away.

'Are you going to work?' asked Sengamalai.

'Yes. I have left some hot tea for you, go drink it,' she said.

'Wait, I will also come with you.'

Kuppan who had stealthily gone to the village to get drunk the previous day, was snoring in a corner, still asleep.

There were only a few women in the workfield that day. Valli was working on a slope, plucking tea leaves, carrying the heavy basket on her back. Her wet sari and drenched blanket added to her discomfort. As she stretched to pick the leaves, she lost her footing and fell down the slope. The other workers carried her to her layyam. That same night she lost her baby. She was down with fever and fits, with no one to care for her as she lay confined to bed.

Someone from her estate had informed her parents of her illness. Immediately, Velan came to see her.

Valli looked thin and wan. Her body had lost its youthful vigour. Velan wept to see his daughter in that state. Even in poverty, there had never been any dearth of love and affection for his daughter, at his home.

The day he came to see Valli, everyone had left for work, except Kamakshi and the little ones. Maruthai had gone to fetch firewood. Valli tried to sit up, but could not.

'If I had known, I would have come earlier,' he said quite agitated and upset.

'Atha, annachi and the rest, are they fine?' asked Valli in a weak voice.

'Your mother is down with fever often. I want Suppan to get married soon, but he is talking about going back to our village. Kakkan is trying to find a girl for him from our village. Let's see,' said Velan.

'Yes, there is no one to help atha, it must be difficult for her. How is Sivakami athai?'

'She is the one who pitches in to help. But her limbs get swollen often and they say it is an incurable disease. Poor thing, it's her fate that she should suffer like this.'

'I must come and see atha, once I get better.'

'She too wants to see you, but she is too ill to come here. Tell me, does Sengamalai look after you well? What about his parents?' He asked.

Valli's eyes fell on Kamakshi. She could not speak the words, but tears ran down her face in anger and frustration. Her sorrows pressed down upon her, and she thought her heart would splinter.

Velan too wept.

'Do you want to come away to our estate?' asked Velan.

'Let me get well, we'll see,' said Valli, as she wept inconsolably. Velan held her close, and comforted her, as he had when she had been a child.

'To hell with him. If you cannot live with him you can come back to us. There are plenty of jobs in our estate,' he told her softly.

Velan stayed on till Kuppan, Sengamalai and Ponnamma returned from work that evening. 'So, what brings you here?' asked Kuppan, surprised to see Velan there.

'The sinna kangany who visited our estate said that Valli has taken ill, so I came to see her. How can I stay away after hearing about her illness? Are you all fine?' He asked.

'We're just fine,' replied Kuppan in a dissatisfied voice.

'Why don't you send Valli to stay with us for a couple of days, once she gets well?' asked Velan.

'As it is, it is difficult to keep your body and soul together. Who is going to pay us for all this gallivanting here and there? Let's see,' said Ponnamma, brusquely.

'I will try to bring her,' said Sengamalai. His mother quelled him with a look.

Velan prepared to leave that very evening.

Valli wept and sobbed, but to no avail.

'I will come again if I can, and I'll bring Suppan along with me,' Velan promised.

After Velan left the entire household was in an uproar. Both Ponnamma and Kuppan abused Valli.

'You wretch, what do you lack over here? Who is ill-treating you? You slut! Wait till I pull your eyes out!' ranted Ponnamma, as she landed a kick on Valli.

'She is nicely fattened, having three meals a day. That's why she behaves like this,' said Kuppan, adding fuel to fire. Sengamalai did not defend his wife.

Maruthai, who was watching this scene began to sing, as he sharpened his knife.

His singing annoyed Kuppan, 'What has come over you? You are becoming insolent.'

Maruthai started laughing.

'Keep quiet, you ass!' said Sengamalai, trying to diffuse the situation.

18

Valli resumed work as soon as she felt better. She had not yet recovered completely. But unable to put up with Kuppan and Ponnamma's abuses she returned to work. The following day she fainted on the field. In spite of that, she went to work the next day.

When the sinna dorai came riding his horse on his daily rounds, he was surprised to see Valli, 'Yesterday you fainted and today you are back at work? Go back to your layyam,' he ordered.

The monsoon season was over and the month of Margazhi had come, bringing the wind and cold weather in its wake. Even though the weather had changed, Valli's life did not change. Ponnamma and Kuppan continued harassing her. 'Is this rice? You call this a curry? How can we eat this?' Kuppan would rant drunkenly. Some days she would be dragged by her hair and beaten up mercilessly. In this manner some months passed by. One day she heard the news that her mother had died. She cried, begged and pleaded, to at least be permitted to see her mother's final remains. But even this was denied to her.

'What if you were away in India? Could you have gone for the funeral?' asked Sengamalai callously.

'What is the matter with you? You are like a stone with no feelings,' she raged at him.

'You dare talk back to me?'

'What else can I do? Do you want me to be like you, an unfeeling stone?' lashed out Valli.

'There is no point in you raging like this. Don't worry, you know they do this to provoke you,' advised Chittu, her neighbour.

'Let them all soon get what they deserve,' cursed Valli.

Valli's sorrow pricked Sengamalai's conscience. But he was conditioned by the fear his father and mother had instilled in him. He knew he would anger his parents if he made any attempts to comfort his wife. But his silence got him in trouble with Valli. Sengamalai was torn by conflicting emotions.

The severe chill of the season pierced one's bones. Sengamalai was despondent. He sat by the faint light of the tin lamp, searching for an answer to his dilemma. But the solution evaded him.

Valli soon gave birth to a beautiful, healthy boy. He was named Murugan. Valli found it stressful, juggling work, caring for her child and also caring for Ponnamma's many children. She woke up at four in the morning and went to bed at eight or nine in the evening, during which time she had to work round the clock.

The situation in the layyam was getting worse everyday. Kuppan would get drunk and pick quarrels with everyone. Besides, he also brought toddy for his wife Ponnamma. This created new problems for Valli.

'Why don't you speak to your mother? Ask her to stop harassing me,' Valli would ask Sengamalai. But this only angered him.

'Just shut up and do your work,' he would say.

'If I don't, what will you do?' she asked.

'I will show you what I will do! You have become very brazen,' he would say and beat her ruthlessly. Their life continued with many such quarrels and bickering.

Valli noticed that Sengamalai was getting increasingly intolerant and aggressive. Valli bore him four children of which only two survived—Murugan and Meenakshi.

One day, she heard the second gong calling them for work. Hurriedly she lifted the baby, hung the basket on her head and went down to the roll-call shed.

'Hurry up, the sinna kangany will scold us for being late,' said Chittu.

'Coming, coming. God, always this scramble!' complained Valli.

'Is Kuppan here?' asked a voice in the dark.

'He just left for the roll-call shed, what do you want?' she asked the person.

'Nothing, the dorai asked me to bring him,' said the man.

'The dorai? What for?' she asked.

'I don't know.'

'You are the dorai's handy man, aren't you? Yes, you wouldn't know?' Valli said sarcastically.

'And you have a big mouth,' said the man, as he left to look for Kuppan in the roll-call shed.

When Valli reached the roll-call shed, they told her that Kuppan had been taken to the office.

During lunch, Sengamalai told her what had happened.

'Dorai called ayya and asked him whether he went to the tavern yesterday. He said that he didn't.'

'Then?'

'He had stolen coffee seeds from the estate to buy toddy. Some fellow has informed the office. This man had brought the bag in which ayya had stolen the coffee.'

'Then?'

'They beat him up and have taken him to the police station.'

'To the police? Just for stealing a few coffee beans?'

'Actually, ayya has stolen often, to get money for his drink. They have found this out, that's why they have sent him to the police station.'

'What will happen now?' she asked.

'Who knows? Only when the fellow who has taken him to the police station returns, will we know.'

The next day the dorai called Sengamalai and told him, 'Your father is a wicked man. He is a thief. We have sent him to prison.

They have given him two years imprisonment.' The periya dorai was an arrogant bully, and no one dared go against him.

'Aiyo! Those sinners, they must have killed my husband! I don't know where they have taken him,' wailed Ponnamma, as she beat her chest.

That evening, when Valli had gone to fetch water she ran into the sinna dorai.

'Sami, please do something for my father-in-law. He has family and children dependant on him,' she pleaded boldly.

Maclean smiled, 'You mind your own business. The beating that you get is enough! Tell me if there is anything you want?'

She was dumbfounded. People living on the plantation – workers, kanganys, kanakapillais and dorais – were a small community by themselves. In that small community there were no secrets. Nothing could happen without everyone knowing about it.

'What is it that you want?' he asked her again.

She was taken aback. After a moment's thought she said, 'I want a room in a different layyam for my family.'

'Alright, we are clearing the forest down the valley, we are going to build a new layyam there, you can have a room,' said Maclean, as he walked away.

During this time, Ponnamma gave birth to a baby, three months after Kuppan had gone to prison. Maruthai started working. He was not like Sengmalai, he was very playful and took nothing seriously. He would sing songs and play cards with his friends. If his mother reprimanded him, he would just beat her up. He was a law unto himself.

It was extremely difficult for two families to live in that single room. After returning from work, Valli had to cook, clean and serve food for the family. She would be given the leftovers, and some days she would have to go to bed even without that. Hunger can be a terrible thing, especially when you have to feed a baby. She felt her knees buckle under her as she climbed the slopes to do her work. Often she sat by the river bank, the only place she had some peace and solitude and cried to herself.

'Hey Valli, what are you doing over here at this time? You should not have come alone! You should have brought Kamakshi.' Hearing the sinna kangany's voice, Valli, taking the water pot hurried home.

'I am talking to you and you are walking away?' asked the sinna kangany.

'What is there to say? The devil is not going to possess me if I come alone,' she replied in an irritated voice and kept walking.

'Not the devil, but a man might want to do that! Why do you have to work so hard? Why don't you tell Ponnamma to make Kamakshi work. She is growing fat day by day and one of these days she will run away with some fellow,' he said, twirling his moustache as he stood barring Valli's way.

'It's none of your business. Let me go, will you?' she said annoyed.

'Why should you be bothered with all this. If you do as I say you can live like a queen,' he said, as he caught hold of her hand. Valli shook him off and tried to walk away.

'Come on Valli, don't put up your price,' he said, as he tried to get closer.

'Chi! Let go of me,' she ordered. By now the kangany caught hold of her waist and tried to draw her to him.

'No one will come here at this time. Don't be afraid, this place is secluded,'

'Chi! Let me go. Don't try all this with me!' she tried to pull her hand away from him.

'Are you trying to escape from me?'

'Leave now or I will scream for help,' she said.

The sinna dorai was just then returning to his bungalow after his usual evening walk. Hearing the scuffle he hurried to the place.

'Kangany, what's going on here?' asked Maclean.

'This girl is teasing me dorai,' muttered the kangany.

'Leave now! In future I don't want to catch you doing these things, understand?' Maclean admonished him.

Bearing a grudge against Valli, the sinna kangany walked away.

'How many times have I told you not to come here so late in the evening,' said Maclean.

'I can fetch water only after I get back from work, what can I do?'

'Never mind, in future try to be early,' said Maclean as he quickly walked away.

Valli was lost in thought. There are good and bad people in all walks of life, she decided. Just as we need rain and sunshine, darkness and light, this world also requires all sorts of people. Valli had lost her childhood naivete a long time ago. She now was a young woman who was emotionally mature, bold in her thinking, and eager for new experiences that life had to offer her.

'Valli, Valli,' Sengamalai's call broke her reverie.

19

In spite of an early marriage, constant harassment and frequent child births, Valli still retained her youthful charm. The kangany, kanakapillai and the young men in the estate were in awe of her beauty. Her long hair and silver ornaments added to her allure. Her breasts were not confined to a blouse, and her tightly wrapped sari highlighted their attractiveness. Ironically, Sengamalai was indifferent to her charm and Valli was ignorant of her own attractiveness.

Valli sat at her doorstep nursing the baby. Murugan was playing in the yard, without a stitch of clothing, despite the cold. Sengamalai was sharpening his pruning knife on a stone and checking its sharpness with his fingers. Meenakshi tugged her father's vetti as she nursed at her mother's breast.

'It will be nice if we plant some banana crop here,' said Sengamalai.

'Here? You know the dorai has strictly said that we cannot plant as we wish in the estate,' said Valli.

'Why not? Why shouldn't we plant some banana, brinjal and some chilly on the side like satan,' said Ponnamma. 'Sengamalai, I think it's time we got your sister Kamakshi married. Find a good boy for her,' she told her son.

'We should consider our cousin Sinna Karuppan's son. He is the only suitable boy here. He is a good worker,' said Sengamalai.

'Unless one get's their daughters married at the right time, one cannot live here with their self-respect intact,' said their neighbour Chittu.

'Not this month, we'll do something about this next month,' said Ponnamma.

Maruthai who was returning after a bath in the river, was singing to himself.

'I saw the periya kangany on the way. He is coming to inspect our layyam. The tea factory construction in the upper division is going to be completed, soon after that, it seems they are going to build a hospital,' Maruthai informed them.

'In that case, why don't you go find some work there?' said Ponnamma to Maruthai.

'I am not working for any fellow, you understand?' said Maruthai vehemently.

Before he could finish talking, they saw the Periya Kangany Kandiah, Sinna Dorai Maclean and the periya dorai walking down the mountain slope.

'The dorai is coming, the dorai is coming!' This caused a stir in the layyam and all the people stood in attention.

'Maclean,' called the periya dorai.

'Yes sir.'

'Ask them to clean this layyam. It is very filthy!' said the periya dorai.

'It is too crowded. There are too many people in this layyam,' said the kangany.

'Yes, he is right,' said Maclean.

Periya dorai looked at the layyam and its residents with distaste.

'Oh, alright. Accommodate some in the new layyam,' he told the kangany.

'Yes dorai!' replied the kangany briskly. He was very proud of the fact that the periya dorai had left him in charge of the estate.

Valli stared at the kangany's smart turnout. His tall well-built figure, his sparkling diamonds, zari turban and spotless white vetti, reminded her of the kanakapillai at Senthur.

The next day Maclean sent for Sengamalai. He went to the office in trepidation, wondering what was in store for him. There were a few others too waiting like him.

'You go to the valley where they are clearing the jungle. You can build the new layyam over there. Plaster the walls with mud and use grass for the roof. If there are any tin sheets left over from building the hospital, you can use them to cover the roof,' instructed the kangany.

'Yes, ayya,' said the workers who were given the instruction.

'Do all this in the evening, after you finish work. He then called a worker, 'Come here! There's some wood lying in the pit there. Use it for the horse's stable at the sinna dorai's bungalow. Call Velusamy the stable hand. Ask him to take the horses to the periya dorai's stable. Go!'

Just then Maclean came out of the office and asked, 'Have you told them everything kangany?'

'I have dorai. But we have to put a watchman there. That place is frequented by wild animals. Especially bison, elephant and fox.'

'Ask them to build a shelter on the tree top and light a fire at night. If you keep beating the drum the animals will go away,' said Maclean.

'We'll do that, we have to see to the welfare of our men,' said the kangany.

'Yes, do the needful,' said Maclean as he left the office.

'Alright, get to work, all of you,' ordered the kangany.

ꟹ

It seems the kangany is going to India next month to bring his wife here,' said a woman.

'That is why they are building a new house for him.'

'He is not like us. What does he not have? He has more authority than the dorai.'

'Don't you know, even the dorai listens to him,' said Chittu.

'Why talk about these big shots?' said Valli.

'Fine. You know the periya kangany has an eye on you. You better be careful,' said Kaveri, winking at Valli meaningfully.

'Can't you keep quiet? Shut your mouth, and stop spreading such gossip,' admonished, an annoyed Valli.

'Listen to her speak! If we tell the truth she says it's gossip. As if she is a naive girl,' said Kaveri with a sneer.

'It is late. All of you get on with your work,' said the sinna kangany. Every time he saw Valli, he was annoyed. The fact that the sinna dorai had caught him red-handed still rankled.

The women hung their baskets on their heads and walked up the hill in a single file. The air was filled with gossip and laughter as they walked to their work-field. The tea bushes were adorned with sparkling dew and the tender green leaves awaited the gentle touch of these women. The women too would get animated on seeing a bush that had put out new leaves. The simple joys in their lives was thus enmeshed with the well-being of these bushes. They were silent companions in whom the women confided their joys and sorrows. If the bushes could speak they would tell a thousand tales.

One day while at work, Valli put her basket down to go to the river for a drink. One side of the slope was covered with thick bushes and on the other side she saw the men clearing the jungle. Suddenly she saw two figures disappear into the bushes.

It was a good thing that they did not see her. She quickly hid behind a tree. Through the branches she saw the kangany embrace Kaveri. She gave up the thought of going to the river and without lingering any longer she just walked back to the field. She heard her baby, whom she had put to sleep in the cloth-cradle, cry for milk. She fed her before going back to work. Just then the sinna kangany came by and looked into her basket, 'Is this all you have picked? And look it's all matured leaves,' he said.

'I haven't removed the stalks yet. I just fed my baby!' she said.

'Is this how you pass your time?' he asked snidely.

'I will finish my work on time,' Valli said, as she hung her basket back on her head.

'Who asked you to pick these mature leaves in the first place? If you wish to work, do it properly!' he admonished her.

'Fine! I will,' Valli said curtly.

The kangany was irritated by her reply and walked off in a huff.

20

Kamakshi was married before her father Kuppan returned from prison. On an auspicious day, four or five families gathered together to get her married to Karuppan's son, Periasamy, who worked on the estate.

'Valli, the work on the new layyam has been completed. But we cannot cover the roof with grass because it is too wet to cut the grass. There are too many snakes and too much water. Only when the sun is out can we do that,' said Sengamalai.

'In that case we will soon get a room, won't we?' asked Valli.

'Yes I suppose so.'

'Chittu said the periya kangany is going to India,' said Valli.

'Let him go to India or to hell, only let him pay our dues and go,' he said in frustration.

'Why, what's happened to our wages?' she asked.

'It's gone towards our unending debts,' said Sengamalai.

'They will give it to you only if you demand it. Otherwise do you think the kangany will give it to you?' asked Maruthai, who was listening to their conversation.

'Well, you are sitting like a stone! Why don't you go to work?'

'I am thinking of going to work at the new factory, where they are going to bring big machines from England to process tea leaves,' he said playfully.

'You mean you are going to wait until then. Why, what's wrong with the work we do?' asked Sengamalai.

'I can see that the picking season has begun and they are thinking of planting more bushes in the lower division. But I'll just wait for the new machines from England. I will think of going to work after they come. Hey Muruga, you would have also grown by then, and we could both go together,' he said smartly, carrying Murugan, Valli's son.

'Do you want us to feed you till then?' asked Ponnamma who was sitting on the doorstep.

'There are women like you on this estate, look at how they make their living. What the earth is finally going to consume, a man can have too, can't he? You should go along with the times and live like the others instead of trying to be chaste goddesses. No one is going to pay you, if you work like this!' Maruthai laughed at them.

Valli stood frozen. Murugan laughed without understanding the full import of what he had said. Valli realised that there was truth in what Maruthai said. Ponnamma remained silent. Sengamalai, at a loss for words, left the room in search of his friend Singaram.

Hearing Meenakshi's cries, Valli lifted the baby from her cradle. Ponnamma's child was crying on the other side, having wet itself. That small room was teeming with children all over the place.

'Athai, the child is crying,' Valli called out to her mother-in-law.

'Why don't you attend to the child? Day by day I see that you are growing too smart for your own good,' said Ponnamma.

Work began in the new factory. The women took their day's picking to the factory shed to be weighed and then returned to their layyam in the evening. The primitive shed with its thatched roof was gone and in its place a larger shed with tin roof was constructed to weigh the tea leaves. The estate was also dotted with smaller sheds. During certain months, when the tea bushes are lush with new leaves, the women would take in their picking, twice a day.

Valli delivered another child which did not survive even a week, and died of undernourishment and insufficient protection against the chill.

The work on the new layyam was completed and Sengamalai told Valli that they would move there soon. This was welcome news for the tired and dispirited Valli. It was bad enough to be shackled to the estate, with no knowledge of the outside world, but it was unbearable to have no peace and harmony in one's personal life as well.

One day, a man working in the store came and told Valli, 'The kangany asked me to bring you along, he wants to see you.'

'What does he want?'

'Who knows,' he replied, giving her a meaningful look.

Valli felt ashamed and angry, 'What does he want?' she asked again.

'Why don't you go and ask him?' he said.

Valli was on her own when she received the message. Ponnamma had gone to the neighbour's, Sengamalai and Maruthai were also away.

Valli followed him and after going some distance he turned and said, 'I am going to my layyam, the kangany will be waiting for you in the field down the valley.'

Valli did not understand the purpose behind this strange request, but still decided to go ahead and find out for herself. She soon saw the Kangany waiting for her.

'Is that you, Valli? What is this, the sinna kangany complains that you pick mature leaves. How can you do that?' he asked with an oily smile on his face. This came as a surprise to Valli, who had never seen him smile.

'I don't pick mature leaves, ayya. If you wish you can check my basket at any time and kick me out of my job if that is true,' she said meekly.

'We don't throw people out for all these little things. Well, will you come down to the lower field tomorrow?' he asked her softly, making his intentions very clear.

'What for, ayya?' she asked him, pretending not to understand.

'Come on Valli, don't to be naive,' he said. Just then they heard the sound of the horse's hooves. The kangany walked away without pursuing this any further.

Valli was relieved to have gotten off so easily. She saw the periya dorai on his horse, riding back to his bungalow. Valli stood aside respectfully, letting him pass.

Valli did not know what to do. Should she listen to the kangany or act as though the incident had not occurred.

When she returned to the layyam, she saw that Kuppan had returned from prison and was seated near the doorway. At first, Valli couldn't recognise him. With sunken eyes, hollow cheeks and unkempt hair, he looked quite frightening.

'Valli, don't you recognise me?' he asked, as a violent bout of coughing wracked his body.

She quickly brought him some water and said, 'Here mama, drink this.'

'Do I look like the old Kuppan? No wonder you didn't recognise me! Where is Ponnamma?' He asked.

'She has gone to the neighbouring layyam. She will be back shortly,' Valli said as she lit the tin lamp. By then Sengamalai and Maruthai walked in.

'Who is this?' asked Sengamalai, not recognising Kuppan in the dark.

'Can't you recognize me?' Asked Kuppan.

Seeing his father in this condition, Sengamalai was deeply affected. He cursed the fates that had brought them to this state.

'Who is that?' asked Ponnamma, as she came in.

'It is our ayya,' said Maruthai.

'Come mama, have some hot rice, come,' Valli invited her father-in-law, feeling pity.

'It is a long time since I had hot rice!'

Kuppan got up, washed his hands and feet, and sat down to eat. He had not even noticed his wife Ponnamma. He was so starved for food that he just shoved rice into his mouth. Murugan, Valli's child, hid behind his mother, frightened by the newcomer.

'Is that Murugan? Come here child,' Kuppan called out to his grandson, once the pangs of hunger were appeased.

Murugan started crying. 'It is your grandfather, go to him,' said Valli.

'Muruga, don't you know your grandfather?' asked Ponnamma.

Seeing another child crawling around, Kuppan asked 'Whose child is that?'

'This one is also ours. He was born three months after you went to jail,' said Ponnamma.

'Oh good! His birth has already brought a lot of luck to his father. I have just returned from prison, I wonder what else he has in store for me?' he said with bitterness in his voice.

21

Valli gave birth to twin boys—Raman and Lakshmanan.

Kaveri, her neighbour, and a midwife kept vigil until she delivered them after great difficulty.

Raman and Lakshmanan grew up amidst the lush ambience of the tea estate.

'Valli, it seems the periya kangany is returning from India,' said Kaveri.

'What does it matter whether he comes or not. We have enough troubles to contend with, we don't need him to add to our woes,' said Valli.

'Do you know, our Chittu is now the kanakapillai's mistress?' said Kaveri.

'Oh, Chittu has replaced the other woman, I suppose.'

'And our tea-maker ayya?'

'Yes, what about him?'

'It seems even he has taken up with Masakollai machan's new bride, Vellachi!'

'Atha, atha, the baby is crying—he fell down,' Murugan came running to inform Valli.

Valli ran inside to attend to the problem.

The periya kangany returned from India with his family and settled in his new bungalow. Next to the periya dorai, and the sinna dorai, it was the periya kangany who was the most important person on the plantation. In fact, it wouldn't be false to claim that he wielded more authority than either of them.

'I have more than two thousand people working in this plantation. It is not child's play, managing the lot. That's why the dorai has given me a horse. This plantation has grown so large now, I told him that it was difficult for me to walk around and supervise. He suggested I learn to ride a horse,' said the kangany.

The Sinna Kangany listened meekly and thought how nice it would be nice if he too was given a horse.

'Yes ayya, your father too was a well-known kangany in his time and you are his son, born and brought up here. Our dorai has much respect for you,' he said in a flattering tone.

'Yes, all that is as long as he gets his work done. Anyway send four workers to my house after they report at the roll-call shed. Send a nice girl to attend to the work at my house. I hear two new girls have come from India.'

'Yes, one is called Vellachi and the other one is her sister. She had to bring her sister along after marriage, for her mother's dead. There was no one to look after the girl.'

'Hmm, you attend to your work here. I will go on my rounds. How is our Valli?'

'She is alright, ayya,' replied the sinna kangany.

The periya kangany walked towards his new house in a pensive mood.

Sengamalai's father was back to his old ways. He would often steal away to the village to drink toddy with his cronies. One night they beat up the watchman. The dorai was furious and sent them all to jail.

The responsibility of taking care of Kuppan's family fell on Sengamalai. Maruthai was being difficult, not listening to anyone and doing as he pleased. The younger ones, Chidambaram and Mangalam, had started to work on the estate. Ponnamma, due to frequent childbirths, had grown weak and now found it difficult to work.

'It is difficult enough running our family, now we have to look out for them too,' Valli said with resentment.

One day, when Valli had gone to get something from her mother-in-law's layyam, Ponnamma picked a fight with her.

'You slut! You conniving bitch! You think your husband jumped from the sky? I am the one who brought him up. Not only did you take him away from his family, but you also grudge what little he gives us,' accused Ponnamma.

'What are you shouting for? Don't I have my own children to care for? You can keep your son to yourself. You want us to starve while you eat and enjoy, I suppose.'

'Don't I know about you, you run around like a young girl. Are you planning on taking up with another man after getting rid of my son?' asked Ponnamma.

'Shut up! You should be ashamed of your words,' replied Valli, furious.

'You slut, you talk like you are a chaste wife! Don't I know you?' shouted Ponnamma as she caught hold of Valli's hair. Valli freed herself from her hold, and spat on her.

'Why should I defend myself? The whole estate is laughing about you sending a young, unmarried girl to work,' sneered Valli.

Hearing this Ponnamma was even more outraged. This intensified their scuffle, until Valli freed herself from her hold and went home crying.

That evening she quarrelled with Sengamalai, 'Ask your mother to keep her mouth shut, will you? Otherwise, god will give her what she justly deserves. Our god Muniyan has, as it is, kept her in this state. Why hasn't she learnt her lesson?' raged Valli.

'Everyday, it is the same old thing. I just have to return from work and you start your tirade. You wear me out with your irritating talk,' said Sengamalai.

'What do you care! I am the one who has to bear the burden.'

'That's enough, just shut your mouth,' he said, as he walked out of the layyam.

'Atha, why are you crying?' Murugan came up to her and wiped her tears. Meenakshi too started crying.

Valli was moved by her children's misery. Though she was heartened by their show of empathy, she did not want them to be saddened.

'Don't cry, atha! You just wait, when I grow up, I will beat up paati,' said Murugan, trying to comfort her. Valli laughed when she heard this, momentarily forgetting her sorrows. She hugged her children close and wondered what the future held in store for them.

Soon after the twins were born, she had another baby, a girl this time, whom she named Anjalai. It was about this time that she received a message from Hamilton Estate that her father Velan had died.

Valli was distraught. She felt that she was now all alone in a hostile world, with no one to truly care for her. Even though it had been many years since she had seen her father, she had the comfort of knowing that there was someone for her somewhere in the world. But now, she felt bereft, as though someone had stolen the only valuable possession she had.

People in the layyam tried to console her. Sengamalai too did his best to comfort her. But Valli's sorrow lay buried deep inside her, leaving a permanent scar.

One day, hearing her cry in her sleep, Sengamalai went to her, 'Don't cry, Valli. Our sons will care for you even more than your father,' he said softly. 'I am here for you, you are not an orphan.' He laid his cheek against hers and whispered gentle words to her. She sought refuge in his comforting arms.

'Valli, I am your father, your mother, your everything, understand?' he pressed against her. The rancid smell of neem oil, the strong odour of sweat emanating from their hard-working bodies, the cold dampness of the mud floor, the icy chillness in the air, all this disappeared and two people under the warmth of the blanket, temporarily forgot their trouble-ridden lives and found happiness together. His calloused hands smoothed down her body, erasing the pain in her heart. The faint light from the tin lamp made the night magical and special.

The night was still, except for the occasional howling of a fox or the crowing of a cock. The gentle rays of the moon floated through the sack-covered doorway. Valli and Sengamalai were woken up by the sound of voices in the dark. They recognised one of the voices as their neighbour Kaveri's.

'I will come again tomorrow after it gets dark. Tell him, I'll be there,' she said.

'He is a big man, don't be late, or he will be angry. Besides, in the night he is mostly drunk and does not know what he does,' said another voice in the dark.

'Ok, you go now,' said Kaveri, as she disappeared into her house.

After this, Valli was unable to go to sleep. She stared at the thatched roof above her and very soon she heard the roll of drums beckoning them to work. Their rested bodies now sprang of life. Another day had dawned.

This time when Kuppan returned from prison he looked worse than before, all skin and bones. He was made to do quarry work in the prison and without proper food, the hard labour had taken its toll on him. His back was badly scarred due to the whipping, and he was in no position to work anymore.

'Mama is coughing badly all the time,' Valli told Sengamalai.

'I asked him to go to the new hospital and get some medicine, but he is unable to climb up the slope to reach the hospital.'

22

Valli stood at her doorstep, delighted with the brinjal, lady's finger and chilly growing in her garden. The pumpkin creeper had spread over the roof and had put out small fruits. This was the first time since she had come to the estate, that she had been able to make a garden for herself.

'You will have plenty of vegetables this year,' said Kaveri, breaking into Valli's thoughts. 'Come, let's hurry, we will be late for the roll call—first siren was sounded long ago,' she said.

Valli took her basket from the door and hung it on her head. She adjusted the sack-cloth she had placed on her head and started out for work.

'Meenakshi, take care of the child. Don't leave her alone. Muruga, don't take the child to the river, understand? The sky looks dark and it might rain, we have flash floods when it rains in the upper ranges,' she instructed her children as she hurried out to meet the other women going to work.

'Hey Chittu, what's the matter with you? Did you quarrel with your husband? Yesterday he was roaring drunk.'

'Nothing new, he is always like that. Did you hear about our Poonjolai?'

'You mean our kangany's wife Poongavanam?'

'Wherever she plants, it blossoms like her name,' said Chittu. Everyone laughed.

'There come Kaveri and Valli. Yesterday, I saw Karuppan machan unable to tear his eyes away from Valli,' said another woman.

'What are you women laughing about?' asked Valli.

'You! People were talking about your sexy walk at the roll-call shed yesterday,' said Chittu.

'You women have no other work but to listen to the gossip of those useless idiots,' said Valli.

'Even the other day I heard the sinna kangany say "Valli is like the tender tea leaves in her basket",' said Kaveri.

'Shut up, you troublemaker,' said Valli.

'You were saying something about Poonjolai, what about her?' a woman asked Chittu.

'Oh that! The secret is now out. You know she had a baby yesterday and that baby is golden-hued like a ripe pumpkin,' said Chittu.

'What is so surprising about that? How do you think her husband, the periya kangany, managed to buy an estate right next to this plantation?' said Kaveri.

'They are not like us, we are worked to our bones and at the end of the day we have nothing to show for it,' said Chittu.

'Listen to her talk like an old woman. When the old men in the estate are actually roaming around like young fellows.'

'Shut your mouth! The periya kangany is coming this way,' said Valli.

The periya kangany walked by leisurely. The women stood aside letting him pass. Like a dorai, he glared at them as he walked away, his face unsmiling and hard.

The kanakapillai came up to him.

'Did you see, the seedlings we planted last year are already putting out new shoots. We should be harvesting them in another two years,' said the periya kangany.

'Yes ayya, our coolies worked hard on this land. Besides, this is virgin soil, naturally the seedlings are doing well.'

'Do you remember what I told you before?' asked the periya kangany, lowering his voice.

'You mean about sending workers to your land? Yes, I remember that.'

'Don't forget! I will be going there tomorrow to take a look,' said the periya kangany, referring to the new land he had bought recently.

'Don't forget to mark these workers present at roll-call before you send them off to work on my land,' said the periya kangany as he hurried to his horse tethered to a tree. He got on to his horse and rode to the upper division just like a dorai.

The women were walking along silently. As soon as the kangany left, they started giggling and making fun of him.

'The old man is really something,' said one woman.

'What is all this talk. Run along now, it is getting late,' the kanakapillai hurried them.

That evening after the women had brought in their day's picking, the sinna kangany asked Valli to stay back.

'Valli, wait awhile, the rest of you can go. Valli, I want you to work in the store for a few days,' he told her.

Valli stood there, not comprehending the situation. The sinna kangany led the reluctant Valli to the store room, and said, 'Valli, I have been interested in you for a long time now.'

'Can't you mind you own business? First it was Chittu, then Kaveri, and now you want me?' asked Valli, angrily.

'Stop acting like you are the goddess of chastity,' said the sinna kangany, as he caught her hand and pulled her to him.

'Let me go or I'll scream!'

'I'll kill you!'

'Who do you think you are? Let go!' she shook him off, and ran as fast as she could.

On the way out she bumped into the periya kangany. Seeing her agitation he asked her, 'What happened?'

'That... That...' she stammered, 'the sinna kangany...'

'You go, I'll take care of this,' he said. He did not look too perturbed.

That was the second time she had stood up against the sinna kangany. She knew that he would make life difficult for her. It happenned sooner than she thought.

The following week he complained that she was picking mature tea leaves. He also reduced the weight of her basket making it look like she had picked less. He complained about her to the sinna dorai.

The sinna dorai took her to task. 'Valli, what is this, the sinna kangany complains that you are not working properly, he says you pick mature leaves, is that true?'

'No dorai, that's not true!' Valli said, emphatically. She undid the basket from her head and let it down. Grabbing some leaves from her basket she showed it to him, 'Look dorai, look for yourself.'

'Hmm, I see,' he said, reflectively.

'Dorai,' said Valli.

'What is it?' he asked.

'Sinna kangany is troubling me too much dorai!' she said picking up courage.

'Alright, you go, I'll see to it,' he said, as he smiled to himself. He could never understand these people's lives no matter how much he tried.

'Damn it all! What nonsense!' he cursed, as he left the place.

She stood there looking at him, till he had gone some distance.

'Why Valli! Your eyes seem to be traveling far?' Kaveri said sarcastically.

'Chi! Keep quiet!'

'As if we don't know! Do you think we don't know? I knew about this long ago. I knew there must be something going on.'

'Shut up, will you?' said Valli, now furious.

'Why are you getting so worked up? Is it your guilty conscience? Why all this anger?' Kaveri baited her.

'I asked you to shut up!' she shoved Kaveri aside.

'Are you looking for a fight?'

Valli caught hold of Kaveri's sari and shook her, 'Keep your mouth shut, you ass!' They caught hold of each other's hair, and fell into a scuffle.

'Look at her anger, the whore,' said Kaveri.

'Why, you are jealous, aren't you?' asked Valli.

They heard the kangany's voice and went back to work.

'What's going on here? Are you playing games or are you picking tea?' shouted the kangany.

The women continued picking diligently with their calloused hands, stained with the juice of tea leaves. Their fingers were nimble and quick, as they skillfully picked the two leaves and a bud. They bent, leaned, straightened, and stretched themselves as they went about their business, swiftly filling their baskets with leaves. On the other side the men were pruning the overgrown tea bushes.

'Hey Muthu, have you finished with your pruning?' asked the sinna kangany.

The lush bushes now stood bare, like a woman shorn off her beautiful tresses.

'Leave those cut branches as they are. Their leaves must be allowed to become compost. You can collect the twigs later for fuel,' ordered the sinna kangany.

'It is time to weigh the tea leaves. Go to the shed,' the kangany ordered the women. The women found it difficult to walk up the mountain with their heavy baskets. They dug their toes to steady themselves on the slope, as they walked single file to the shed. Some had overflowing baskets and carried the excess tucked away in their sari.

'What a lot of tea leaves in that field,' said a woman, as she put down her basket. The women dropped the leaves from their basket, on to the floor and removed the mature leaves and stalks that they had picked in their haste.

The kangany in-charge of weighing the leaves, came in and started weighing and writing the account for each woman. He gave a slip to them that was to be handed to the office.

'I picked ninety pounds yesterday,' said Chittu.

'I picked ninety-nine pounds, you know!' said Valli with pride. They did not worry over the fact that they were not the people who were going to benefit from their hard work.

'It will be nice to return to the layyam, and have some food before feeding the baby,' said Kaveri. The fight with Valli still rankled her.

'I only had some tea this morning before I rushed to work,' said Chittu.

'This is the tea-picking season,' said Valli.

The fragrance of the tea leaves hung on them as they returned to their layyam after work.

23

'Ramu, where are you? Where is Lakshmanan?' Valli called out to her son. Raman was now seven years old.

'There he is, he is with annachi. They are planning to steal some jack fruit, they are going to be beaten up when they get caught,' said Raman.

'Did you water the brinjal plants? Did Murugan soften the earth around the cabbage plants?' asked Valli, as she removed her basket and hung it on the door.

'Akka has hoed it. It is two days since Maruthai chithappa left the house and he has not returned,' said Raman.

'Not returned? He must have got drunk and must be lying somewhere in the village.'

'Kaveri athai asked us not to walk on this side.'

'She will say that! It is her father's property, you see.'

'That place where you have planted brinjal is hers, she says.'

'Yes, the dorai has willed it all to her!' Valli said sarcastically.

'I am the one who wanted to plant some vegetables over there. Is it your land?' said Kaveri, who had overheard the conversation.

'Alright woman, stop it,' replied Valli.

'You first shut up. You talk as if you are the doraisani.'

'You can't stand it, can you?' retorted Valli. They stared hostilely at each other, until Valli turned away to go to the river to fetch water.

'Atha, let me also come with you,' said Raman.

'No, you look after Anjalai,' said Valli.

On her way she saw the sinna dorai returning to his bungalow after his evening walk.

'Valli, how are you?'

'I am fine. Ayya, can you give a job for my son Murugan, at the store?' Nowadays, the workers on the plantation talked to the sinna dorai quite freely. He had almost become a father figure to them, quietly listening to their joys and woes. They had great respect for him, coupled with fear and trust.

'Alright, ask Sengamalai to see me,' said the sinna dorai.

That evening, Valli told Sengamalai about the conversation with the sinna dorai.

'You have to talk to the periya kangany before registering his name. You better tell him about it. Why don't we send our Raman and Lakshmanan to school?'

'What? Did you say school? Are you mad?'

'It will be nice if they can learn to read and write, then we can ask the dorai to give them a job in the office,' she said, her voice laced with hope and enthusiasm.

'There is no school in the village. Our tea maker's children go to the town for their schooling. Besides, we have barely enough for our daily sustenance. You think we have money for school?' said Sengamalai, in frustration.

'Why don't you try asking the dorai?'

'I cannot ask him. If you wish, you speak to him.'

'What does it matter to you, let your children be harassed and die like the rest. Only if something like that happens will you learn your lesson,' Valli replied in anger.

'That's enough! You think our children are going to study and become officers! Why don't you just shut up?'

'Will you ask or not?'

'Alright, let us see. Maruthai has just returned. It has been difficult in my mother's house too. He is the only fellow who goes to work. With all these problems, why should we add to our burdens.'

'Somehow if we could just educate them, even if we have to starve, we can worry about the rest later. We will always have difficulties. Raman is intelligent, he should be able to study well,' she said with a sigh.

Outside, Kaveri and the Kangany's lame brother-in-law, Karuppan, were talking to each other. Valli knew he was a cunning man. If he came to the layyam, there was usually something behind the visit. Seeing Valli by her doorway he said, 'I'll get along then. Ask Perumal to come and see me!' and walked away.

'The lame creep! He is just as crooked as his leg!' muttered Valli, under her breath.

'The kangany is bad enough, but this lame fellow is twice as bad. He writes twice the amount of false accounts as the kangany. He takes the extra money and drinks toddy. The kangany's wife, his sister, helps him. Isn't that enough?' said Sengamalai.

'I was told that even two days ago the kangany visited Vellachi's layyam and the kangany's wife beat him up with the broom,' said Valli.

'Well, I am going to see Pandyan. Where is Meenakshi?'

'She has gone to your mother's house, taking Anjalai with her.'

After talking to the kangany and the dorai, Sengamalai got a job for Murugan in the tea factory.

'In another year our Meenakshi too can go to work,' said Valli.

'I asked the dorai about sending Raman and Lakshmanan to school. He said I could do so if I wished. I don't know where we are going to find the money.'

'Take my earrings and sell them. Use the money to put them in school.'

Just as Valli instructed, Sengamalai sold her earrings, and on an auspicious day took the two boys to the town school and enrolled them.

They were ridiculed on the plantation for this.

'She is going to become a big doraisani, her son is going to become an important clerk.' They jeered and made fun of her. But Valli never vacillated from her decision.

She did not worry about those small children walking seven miles to school everyday. She would get up early and pack lunch for them. Sengamalai took them to school for a week.

Even after the children got used to going on their own, Sengamalai got into the habit of going to town with some of his friends and returning home very late. This caused a new problem for Valli.

The rainy season came. It rained continuously, day and night, without respite. The workers found it extremely difficult to walk on those slushy mountain slopes. Their feet got stuck to the mud and slush. They went out to work in spite of the incessant downpour, proliferating leeches, mosquitoes and the severe chill. But having lived in these estates for so many years they had got used to these conditions.

As usual, Ponnamma went to work in the pouring rain. The earth beneath her feet was slushy and wet.

'Your daughter-in-law seems to be very arrogant!' said a woman to Ponnamma.

'He was a good boy, my son. But she twists him around her fingers and makes him dance to her tune,' complained Ponnamma, as she picked tea.

That day they were put to work in the upper division. Ponnamma adjusted her basket and turned, only to find that she had lost her footing. She grabbed at the tea bushes but the tender stems snapped and she slipped and fell down the slope, hitting her head on the root of a casuarina tree.

'Aiyo! Aiyo! Ponnamma has fallen down the slope...she has fallen down!' the women screamed for help.

'What is it? What happened?' the sinna kanganny hastened to the scene, hearing the commotion.

'Ponnamma has fallen off the slope,' the women told him.

'Kanda, Mooka, all of you come here,' he called for help. They carried her to the plantation dispensary.

'Valli, your mother-in-law fell down the slope and she has been taken to the dispensary,' informed Chittu at the weighing shed.

Valli quickly weighed her basket and rushed to the dispensary. By then a messenger had been sent to Sengamalai and he was already there.

'Atha has been badly hurt,' said Sengamalai.

'How did it happen?'

'She slipped and fell down the slope.'

'Will she survive?'

'I don't know! The doctor has asked us to wait.'

'We seem to suffer from one trouble after another. I wonder if our goddess Pappathi is displeased with us,' mused Valli.

Days passed by and Ponnamma could not get up.

'Her backbone is broken. She cannot get up or do any work. She will be bedridden,' said the doctor at the dispensary.

'Who can afford to take care of atha now?' said Sengamalai resentfully.

'After all this time only yesterday you brought home a kid goat. You better make a vow to offer it to our god Karuppan. He is the only one who can save us,' said Valli.

'I think it might be better if Raman and Lakshmanan stop going to school,' said Sengamalai.

'You have to make an issue of this everytime we speak,' Valli said angrily.

Raman was reading in a corner by the light of a smoky tin lamp. He was quiet and intelligent. Lakshmanan was the opposite—a scamp with carefree attitude towards life. Raman with his calm, composed ways reminded Valli of her father Velan.

'He is like my ayya!' she would say.

'Yes, even his face looks like his. Lakshman is like Maruthai, a good-for-nothing, running wild. He is not going to study anything,' said Sengamalai.

'Why? Don't I look like I can study?' asked Lakshman.

Raman did not pay any attention to their conversation. He was engrossed in his writing. Valli went and sat by him and asked, 'What are you writing?'

'I am writing the alphabet, see,' he showed his writing to his mother. She took it in her hands and peered at it, not understanding anything. 'No atha, you have to look at it this way,' he said, laughing at her ignorance. She brimmed with pride, as though her son had already completed his education.

'Meenakshi! Have you cooked the rice?' Valli noted that Meenakshi too was fast growing up.

'We should register Meenakshi as a worker soon. She can cut grass,' said Sengamalai.

'She will only be harassed by those bullies. Let her wait awhile and after she gets married she can go to work,' said Valli.

'If she can't earn a few rupees who will marry her? Unless she knows how to pick tea leaves, no one will marry her,' said Sengamalai.

'Anyway, let us see,' said Valli, with a sigh.

24

The rainy season came to a close, but not Valli's problems. One day, Meenakshi having brought lunch for Valli at the work-field, informed her, 'Our goat has been taken away. It seems the goat had eaten up the plants in Kaveri's garden. I was watching it all the time and it did not eat her plants,' Meenakshi was agitated.

'Kaveri has been eyeing my goat for a long time. Who took the goat away?'

'That lame fellow, Karuppan. He's been hanging around the place from morning.'

'I knew it. That slut Kaveri, did not come to work today. Alright, you go, I will come home and sort it out.'

That evening, she returned home from work to find that Sengamalai was getting ready to go out.

'Do you know they have taken away our goat.'

'I told you something like this would happen!' said Sengamalai.

'Go and speak to the kangany about this.'

'Do you think I have no other work? If you wish, you go talk to him. I am going to the town,' he said.

'You keep saying you are going to town, whatever is there in that town! Oh, let her go to hell. I had vowed that goat to god Muniyan. He'll take care of her,' cursed Valli. The antagonism against Kaveri grew steadily.

Hearing Valli curse, Kaveri's husband Perumal came to pick a fight.

'You talk too much! As if it's not enough that your goat has eaten our plants, you have the audacity to speak foul of my wife,' shouted Perumal.

'You keep quiet. Who spoke to you?' Valli shouted back at him.

'Your goat has destroyed all my brinjal plants, who'll answer for that,' asked Kaveri in rage.

'Muniyan will give people what they deserve. I had vowed the goat to him,' said Valli.

'Why do you waste your breath talking to that useless fellow!' said Sengamalai.

'Chi! You dog! What did you say?' Perumal came towards Sengamalai, ready to fight him. Sengamalai was ready for him. He stretched his hand and pulled out the pruning knife from the thatched roof.

'You just lay your hand on me and I will cut you up with this,' Sengamalai raised his knife.

The people from the layyam intervened and separated them.

'The scoundrel, the bastard!'

'As if we don't know about you!' said Perumal.

By then the kangany who was on his way home, heard the commotion and came to enquire into the matter. 'What is all this noise here?' he asked in his commanding voice.

'This woman lied about my goat, and it's been taken away.'

'It has eaten all the brinjal plants in her garden, and Sengamalai, you cut leaves from the murungai tree to feed your goat, didn't you?' the kangany accused him. Like the anger that flashed on his face, his diamond earrings flashed in his ears.

'I swear I didn't do it. Someone has lied to you!' said Sengamalai.

'Who needs your promise? Karuppan showed me all the cut branches he found in your garden.'

'I swear to you, I did not pluck even a single leaf from the murungai tree.'

'Let those who spread these lies rot! Let cholera take them!' said Valli.

'Why are you so outraged?' asked Kaveri.

'It is you who is envious,' said Valli.

'Alright! Alright! But no one is allowed to rear goats on this estate henceforth,' decreed the kangany, and left the place.

Although the quarrel had stopped that day, the anger and animosity between them did not cease. Everytime Valli saw Perumal's face she felt enraged. Kaveri decided that she would plot to separate Sengamalai from Valli. In this manner, days and months passed by.

That year, the summer was extremely hot. The tea leaves could not withstand the heat. It was the same in India, and due to the extreme conditions, there was a famine. The famine forced thousands of workers to migrate to Ceylon to work on the plantations. Better ships and trains were now available, making the journey less tedious than during the earlier times.

That year, the cholera epidemic was brought to Ceylon from India. It spread across the country like wildfire. The new workers carried this disease wherever they went. That was how cholera came to Rasikollai Rasa Estate. Men died in thousands, like the flies that threw themselves into the fire.

The cholera that had come to Rasa Estate also visited Valli's layyam. Valli, Sengamalai, Murugan, Meenakshi and Raman were affected, but Raman was the only one who succumbed to it.

Their neighbour Kaveri lost her husband. Sengamalai's mother, Ponnamma, and one of his sisters too did not recover from this affliction. Almost every family had lost at least one person to this deadly disease.

The planters, the kangany, the kanakapillai and their assistants never came to the layyams or visited the sick. They were afraid of being infected. The planters got medicines from England to protect themselves from the infection.

Valli's whole life changed with the loss of Raman. They had buried him under the tea bush, near the others who had died in the family. She felt as if a part of her had died with him. All the hope that she had built on him had been washed away. Raman had been her only hope—the one who was to redeem them from their life of slavery and desperation. With his death she watched that dream become an impossibility.

She sat by the tea bush where Raman was buried and stared at it vacantly. The bush, like her child had once been, looked young and hearty, putting out new green leaves. She beat her chest and unable to quell the sorrow from her heart, she sobbed uncontrollably. As though sympathising with the grieving mother, the bush shed its dewdrops like tears. The evening mist descended on the estate and darkness crept in like a cloak. She shivered in the cold.

'Get up, get up!' She heard a voice and looked up. She saw the sinna dorai standing there, tall like a casuarina tree. In that dim evening light, his blue-green eyes looked mysterious. Valli got up slowly. 'Go, go to your layyam. This is not the time to be here. You must not grieve like this,' he spoke the words with a catch in his voice.

Valli could not answer him. Her throat felt constricted by the pain she felt. She sobbed as if her heart was irreparably broken.

'Death is a part of life. You should not be thinking of it. Go now!' he said.

Without looking up, she walked back to her layyam.

The people on the plantation accepted death as an ordinary occurrence. In their unhappy and slavish lives, where there was no room for humanity or compassion, they accepted death like it was a gift from heaven.

'Atha, don't cry! We are all there for you,' said Murugan, comforting her.

'Don't cry like this Valli! After all, what have we lost in this miserable life of ours?' Sengamalai consoled her. Day by day she slowly accepted her fate.

That year she had another child, a girl, whom she called Thailammai.

'Why do I need another child now?' Valli said unhappily.

'What are we to do with the child that has been born?' asked Sengamalai.

25

There were some important changes in Valli's life and family. Lakshmanan stopped going to school. They looked for a groom for Meenakshi. The workers were able to go to the village more freely than before. Because of this, they were able to find a boy from the Serpentine Estate, a neighbouring plantation, and got Meenakshi married with minimum expense. Meenakshi left to live with her husband.

Sengamalai went to the toddy tavern often and had become a habitual drinker. He took the vegetables from the garden and sold them in the village to pay for his drink. Valli was aware of his addiction and tried to check him.

One day, it was very late, and the children had gone to sleep. Murugan sat by the doorway chewing betel. Valli sat by the kitchen fire warming herself. The smoke from the firewood swirled around their room with no way out. It gave a certain warmth to the room.

'What are you doing in that smoke, atha?' Murugan asked his mother.

'The firewood is damp and wet. I hope it dries in the smoke,' Valli coughed as the smoke got to her.

'What's happened to ayya? The nine o'clock gong had already been sounded and he's still not here,' said Murugan.

'He must be lying somewhere, drunk,' said Valli.

After a little while they heard someone singing aloud as he staggered along the pathway.

'That must be ayya,' said Murugan, as he went out to see who it was.

'Oh, the toddy tavern keeper...' sang Sengamalai, then hiccupped, laughed and continued singing, 'you deceptive cheater...'

Staggering, Sengamalai reached the layyam. Murugan was dumbstruck.

'Hey, who is that fellow' Sengamalai shouted in a drunken haze.

'Why are you picking on him?' asked Valli, as she got up and came out.

'Is that my darling Valli? Come here will you? I want to see your sugary face,' he stretched out his hand to reach for her. Valli felt disgusted looking at this new Sengamalai.

'Go sleep, will you? Muruga, help him to bed,' said Valli, moving aside.

'Muruga? Who is that? I don't want Murugan or any fellow... you are my darling, Valli. You come here, you are my beautiful woman,' he once again reached out for her.

'Chi! Get away. You are not a human being. Coming here drunk at this hour of the night, and acting in this shameless manner! Are you not ashamed?'

'Ashamed? Why should I be ashamed to be with my wife? Muruga, isn't that funny?' he laughed.

'Come appu, come. Lie down,' said Murugan in a placating tone, trying to diffuse the situation.

'You think I am drunk? Not at all. Look I am still steady!' Sengamalai crashed on the mat that was spread on the floor. In a short while they heard him snoring. Valli too slept peacefully after that.

ɞ

The sinna dorai had given a job for Murugan in the tea factory. He worked skillfully on the machines that processed and ground the tea leaves.

Valli was surprised to find her son Murugan, all grown up and ruggedly handsome. He had inherited her looks. With a wide forehead, long curly hair, an appealing smile and sparkling eyes, he looked very handsome. Conscientious in his work, everytime he left for work with his pruning knife, Valli watched him with pride.

Periya kanakapillai's brother-in-law, Thangavel, was appointed as the new kanakapillai at the store. Like all kanganys and kanakapillais, he also possessed lying and cheating talents. He too adopted the method of making money by stealing tea from the factory.

After Murugan finished his work in the factory, Thangavel would ask him to go to his house and work there.

The kanakapillai's daughter, a winsome girl of about fourteen, would often follow him around while he worked. Murugan too was not averse to her good looks. She was fairly goodlooking, with a round face, beautiful questioning eyes, long straight hair and a bronze complexion. Wearing pavadai and thavani, tinkling bangles and silver anklets, she presented a pretty picture. The gold necklace and earrings further added to her attractiveness. Murugan was very aware of this young beauty.

'Shall I bring you some rope?' Her question brought him back to earth.

'Where do you want it tied?' he asked her falteringly.

She came near him and showed him the place. It was beyond his reach.

'Have you got a ladder?'

'There is no ladder but you can stand on this box to reach it.'

The box slipped and he fell down. She laughed out loud. Hearing the racket her mother called out, 'Deivanai, what happened?'

'Murugan fell down,' she said.

'Is that why you laughed?' her mother asked her.

Murugan gave her an irritated look, completed his job and thought to himself, 'All these rich girls are quite arrogant.'

'Don't be angry with me,' she said.

He looked at her in surprise. He saw that she was not arrogant as he thought her to be, she was just childish. He saw affection in her eyes.

'Why should I be angry?'

'I shouldn't have laughed at you.' He could see that she still found it funny and was controlling her mirth.

'A mischievous girl,' he thought to himself. On his way home, the incident played many times in his mind and he laughed to himself.

Deivanai, he knew, was an unattainable fruit. She was a kanakapillai's daughter, and he was a poor labourer's son. But can love understand reason? The love and affection that grew in his heart could not be suppressed. Deivanai's affectionate talk and her tinkling laugh attracted him to her. He decided that he must somehow overcome the barriers and make her his wife. He knew he could not speak about this to anyone, nor did he wish to.

They met at the kanakapillai's house when he went to work there and slowly they started meeting near the tea bushes.

'Deivanai, I don't think I can marry you. Your father would not let me,' said Murugan. They sat under the tea bushes, on the damp fragrant earth. He undid the cloth tied round his head, and laid it out for her, so that she could sit comfortably. Her smooth hands and soft body made him heady. He had never seen hands like hers. The workers on the plantation had rough, calloused hands. He touched each finger and felt its softness. This brought him an unfathomable joy and pain, that he could make no sense of.

'Deivanai, you are not going to let me down, are you?' he asked in a quivering voice.

'No, I promise. I am ready to come away with you.' She pressed her face to his shoulder and leaned against him. He got goosebumps just holding her.

'I am a poor labourer. I can give you nothing. You will have to live in the layyam.' Considering the severe austerity of his life he feared for her welfare.

'I don't mind living anywhere, as long as I do not have to marry that lame fellow.'

'I will not let him touch you! I will cut him up with my pruning knife,' Murugan said in anger.

'It has become dark, your mother will look for you. You better go. I will see you tomorrow,' he said. But she did not wish to move out of his embrace, she just held him closer.

Their hearts became one. The fragrance of the tea bushes enfolded them. The cold wind made them shiver. In his embrace she did not feel the unpleasantness of the cold air.

From somewhere they heard a voice calling out to her, 'Deivanai! Deivanai!' She rushed back home.

Murugan returned to his layyam.

After a couple of days Murugan went to the village. When he returned, Valli did not recognise him.

'Muruga, is that you? What happened to your hair?'

'I have cut it,' he said shyly.

Valli looked at her son with awe and pride. At the same time she wondered about these changes in him and felt a shiver of apprehension.

Anjalai came running from inside and laughed at her brother, 'Anna, what is this?'

One day, Deivanai told Murugan that her father was arranging a marriage between her and the kangany's lame brother-in-law, Karuppan. She was distraught and anguished.

A few days later there was a rumour on the estate that Murugan and Deivanai had eloped.

Valli was stunned by the news. Sengamalai in his drunken stupor did not think much about it. But Valli feared that her family might have to face the repercussions of this act.

'You must have been an accomplice to this!' accused the kangany, as he threatened Valli.

'She knew nothing about this,' said Kaveri coming to her defense. After Perumal's death, Valli and Kaveri had buried their enemity.

'What do you know about this, you shut up!' the kangany said menacingly.

'I swear I knew nothing about it,' said Valli.

'Who wants you promises? As if you did not know anything about this. You must have told them to elope.'

'With god as my witness, I did no such thing, ayya. If you wish I will swear on my children!' said Valli, almost in tears.

They informed the police and after four days they traced them and dragged them back to the estate.

The news that Murugan and Deivanai were brought to the office by the police, spread across the estate. On hearing this, Valli ran to the office with her basket.

The periya dorai, sinna dorai, periya kangany and the rest had gathered over there. Deivanai was shaking with fear.

Murugan stood there, his head held high, staring at them fearlessly.

'We have to thrash him up properly so that no one would dare do something like this again,' said the kangany, angrily.

Valli pushed through the crowd and came forward. Seeing the handcuffed Murugan she started weeping.

'Please let my son go. Dorai, please! Give him another chance. He will not do it again. He will not go near that girl. Please, dorai,' she fell at his feet and pleaded with him.

'Atha, keep quiet. Don't ask any favours from them,' said Murugan.

'You fool! After what you have done, you dare talk?'

'Yes, it is I who am talking! Why should I not marry Deivanai, tell me that?'

'How dare you ask to marry my daughter!' shouted the kanakapillai, as he raised his hand to thrash Murugan.

'Ayya, ayya, don't hit him!' Deivanai stopped her father.

'Chi! You ass! Go away! I will cut you up in pieces and bury you! An ungrateful child is better dead than alive. I will see to him first and then deal with you. Shameless dog!' Her father pushed her to the ground.

'Atha, look after Deivanai,' said Murugan. His veins twitched with anger. He suppressed himself, knowing that anger was futile.

They marched Murugan to the police station.

'Look after Deivanai until I return. See that nothing happens to her,' he requested his mother. Murugan paused to look at Deivanai for a minute and was then led away.

Seeing that they were going to take him to the police station, Deivanai panicked. She caught hold of his legs and refused to let him go. She feared for his safety.

'Take me with him. I will also come,' she cried aloud like a child, kicking her legs. Valli tried to pacify her but her father pushed her aside and dragged his daughter home.

Three or four men removed her by force.

'Ayya! I will die! I will kill myself,' she screamed. The mountains echoed with her cries. Tears flowed down Murugan's face.

'Atha, look after Deivanai!' Murugan repeated once again.

'Please, let my son go. Dorai, please. I have no one but him!' she begged. Deivanai's cry pierced her heart but she was powerless.

'I can do nothing! It is not our problem!' said the dorai.

'This is not the time to cry,' Kaveri consoled Valli.

Because of the shock, Valli gave birth to a baby boy prematurely.

They tried to get Deivanai married to Karuppan. But the kangany's wife could not bear the thought of her brother marrying a girl who had eloped with a lowly labourer. She vehemently opposed the marriage.

Deivanai resolved to throw herself into the river, rather than marry Karuppan. It soon became apparent that Devanai was three months pregnant. This news spread on the estate like wildfire. The kanakapillai felt disgraced by his daughter. He thrashed her black and blue, and even her mother couldn't stop him.

Deivanai painfully dragged herself to Valli's layyam. Valli, seeing her at her doorstep, was surprised 'What are you doing here, Deivanai?' she asked.

'I am not going back to my house. I am going to stay here!' said Deivanai and fainted.

26

'Valli give me half a rupee, will you?' asked Sengamalai.

'What do you want it for?'

'As if you don't know! To go to the village, what else?'

'You have ruined the family frequenting the toddy tavern,' she said, exasperated.

'Just shut up! Are you going to give me the money or not?'

'I don't have any.'

'Let us see if you have any or not!' He pulled her sari, looking for money. Deivanai who was working by the kitchen fire, cowered with fright.

'If I don't give it to you, what will you do?'

'Just watch me!' he said, as he started kicking her. He snatched her betel pouch and helped himself to whatever change he could find.

'Give it back to me!' cried Valli. Shaking her off easily, he took the money and left.

The crying Valli noticed that Deivanai was sitting in a corner, crouched in fear. She resolved to get a separate room for her in another layyam.

The next day, when she saw the sinna dorai on his rounds she called out to him.

'What is it Valli?'

'I heard you are going away to England.'

'Yes.'

'When will you return?'

'It could take a long time.'

'Can you please give a room in the layyam near the store for Murugan, dorai?'

'Why? Is Sengamalai troubling you too much?' he asked with a smile.

'Yes dorai! He drinks too much these days.'

'Alright, I will ask the kangany to give Murugan a room.'

'You will be blessed dorai!' said Valli, gratefully.

He dismissed her with a smile and stood there thoughtfully. He removed his hat and wiped the sweat off his face with a kerchief. He gazed around the plantation. A cool breeze brought relief to the hot day. Standing by the tea bushes he looked up into the sky.

The war had begun and he had been summoned to join the ranks. Leaving this peaceful and comfortable life he had to go fight a war. He might even have to sacrifice his life for his country. He pulled out the letter ordering him to enlist from his pocket and read it once again.

He knew that the sacrifice he was going to make was for his country. He then thought of the thousands of labourers working on the plantation. He wondered if they too were, in a way, martyrs. Leaving behind their native villages, their kith and kin, they had come to this country to escape the famine. Here, they sacrificed their lives for the prosperity of the estate. He was disgusted by this fact, and he felt pity and compassion for his workers.

He was aware of the hardships Valli had to undergo since she came to live on the estate after her marriage. She was not the only one—he knew that there were thousands like her who shared her plight.

The afternoon siren roused him from his reverie. He walked back to his bungalow hidden among the bushes.

Three months later, Murugan returned from prison. He was surprised to see Deivanai in the layyam. Valli narrated the events that had taken place after he was put in the prison. They went to a nearby temple in the village, where Murugan married Deivanai.

It was during this time that they got the news that the world war had begun. The whole country was in turmoil.

The sinna dorai got ready to return to England and join the war.

27

As soon as they heard the news that the sinna dorai had left for England, the workers on the plantation became apprehensive. They wondered how the periya dorai was going to manage the plantation on his own. They feared that the reins of the management would be given to the kanganys and kanakapillais.

The rainy season that year was really bad and it took its toll on the labourers. It rained incessantly, the river was in spate, and the floods destroyed much of the crops. Besides, the war brought about scarcity of food, including rice. The kanganys and kanakapillais increased the prices of all the essentials. Even the blanket prices were raised. They shifted the blame for the rising prices on the war. The periya dorai simply turned a blind eye, pretending not to know what was going on.

Valli's family too felt the pinch. Whether it was rain or sunshine, Sengamalai never failed to visit the tavern. He went to work infrequently. Murugan, Lakshmanan and Anjalai worked on the plantation to contribute towards the household expenses. Kumaran and Thailammai, Valli's little ones were also growing up fast.

Lakshmanan was quite different from the other lads in the plantation. Quiet and reserved, he hardly spoke much. After work he returned to their layyam and kept to himself. He was often immersed in thought, but it was apparent that he did not wish to share it with others.

'Lakshmana, what are you thinking about?' Valli would ask.

'Nothing,' he would reply curtly. He was not violent like his father and did not have his bad habits. He did not even have a temper like Murugan.

'It is a pity I did not educate Lakshmanan, that is the mistake I made!' Valli would often say, berating herself.

'Lakshmana, why are you like this? Why don't you join the other boys on the plantation in their revelry. They are going to dance the oyilattam,' said Murugan.

'Dance! Like we need dance in our slavish lives,' he muttered.

'Why are you talking like this?'

'What else do you want me to say? We are slaves aren't we? Whether you wish to call yourself that or not, you know we are not given proper wages for our work. Do they even allow us to move around freely?' asked Lakshmanan with resentment.

'What kind of talk is this? It was always like this, this is nothing new. We cannot change anything now, can we?' said Murugan.

'Why can't we change it? We are so many, why can't we change the few who are ruling us?'

'Enough! Enough! We don't want any more trouble. Our Chithappa Maruthai used to talk like this and he just disappeared one day without telling us. Don't tread his path,' said Murugan.

'No, I will not run away like him. If I have to leave, I will first chase these fellows out before I go!' he declared vehemently.

Just then Sengamalai staggered into the room, dripping wet and hopelessly drunk.

'Why ayya, why do you come home drunk like this?' asked Murugan.

'That is all the solace I have, it gives me comfort. After working for years don't you think my body needs some sort of succour? After some time, you too will start drinking. When we die what have we left behind? Nothing, yes, nothing... Absolutely nothing...they will strip this two yards of rag off me and bury me under the tea bushes. They will be happy about saving money on fertilisers,' he laughed joylessly and sat by the fire in the kitchen, still dripping wet.

Sengamalai had never spoken like this before. Everyone looked at him in surprise and listened to what he had to say.

'There is truth in what he says!' thought Valli to herself.

'As long as you live, live big and then die. Whatever happens, our life is going to remain the same. Why should we worry about it?' Sengamalai advised his sons.

Valli was astonished to hear Sengamalai speak in this manner.

'Is it not enough that you have lost your senses, why do you want to spoil the boys too? You just throw away our money on your drinks,' complained Valli.

'Oh, we are going to be able to build a house with the money we earn! Just go, will you?' Sengamalai mocked at her.

Lakshmanan found his father's logic amusing.

'Atha, why do you worry about ayya drinking? What have we got to lose? It's not like we are going to have more comforts,' said Lakshmanan.

'Do you want him to borrow money and drink? It is so degrading and humiliating!'

'Shame? What is that? People like us cannot afford to have a sense of shame. If we do, then how can we live?' asked Lakshmanan.

'Why don't you also go with him and get drunk?' said Valli, annoyed.

That night Valli could not sleep. The rain poured in torrents, accompanied by thunder and lightning.

The storm outside found an echo in her inner turmoil. She woke up twice to nurse the crying baby, but her thoughts continued to weigh upon her. Lakshman's talk left her anxious. A life of poverty is not always conducive to comprehending the fine distinction between good and evil. But instinctually she had so far led a principled life. These new thoughts and changes had no place in her life.

She must have dozed off. It was nearly dawn. The rain now was a mere drizzle.

Valli was suddenly awakened by some strange sounds in the dead of the night. She woke to find that her bed was completely drenched. But her tired body and mind did not let her get up and shift. She removed the child from her breast and it began to whimper in protest.

Once again Valli was disturbed by the voices coming from Kaveri's room. She saw the sack cloth hung over her doorway, flap in the wind and heard a sudden thud. She woke up from her mat to check on the disturbance.

She clearly heard Kaveri's voice say, 'Go away! Don't come near me. I have enough trouble, I don't want any more from you. Go, go!'

'Only this once, please,' pleaded a male voice. There was no doubt about it, it was Sengamalai's voice. She turned around and looked at Senagamalai's bed in the dark. The bed was empty. A sharp pain pierced Valli's heart. She sat down, numbed by the turn of events. The baby still cried, but she couldn't attend to it.

Her mind raced in different directions. She knew that it was almost impossible to refuse the kangany or the kanakapillai—but what about ordinary people like Sengamalai?

She was thoroughly disillusioned and disgusted with the world.

She heard another thud by her doorstep.

'Who is that?' she asked in rage. She knew it was Sengamalai.

Sengamalai grunted.

'Where did you go in this rain?'

'I went to relieve myself.'

'Where, inside Kaveri's room?'

'No!'

'Chi! Shut up! Are you a man? What business do you have in her room? With your pitiable earnings you want another woman, do you?' she asked, boiling with rage. She felt wretched.

Another day dawned. The first siren had gone off. The rain too ceased. Rasikollai Rasa Estate saw the beginning of another day.

28

'Atha, atha! What baby is it?' Murugan eagerly asked from the door-way. Deivanai could be heard moaning inside.

'A boy, of course!' said Valli, bubbling with joy.

'A boy, is it? Thank god, there will be less trouble!'

'Why, do you suppose a boy is going to bring you money and a girl will not be earning her own? Be it as it may, they are all asses.'

'Even so, I don't have to guard him with care.'

'What name have you chosen for the child? Let it be a good, modern name and also a god's name,' Valli said.

The infant began to cry, and Valli went in to attend to it.

The baby was born during the rainy season and was affected by the cold and the damp. Their room at the new layyam was protected by a tin roof, and a sack cloth in place of a door.

Murugan lovingly named his first-born Marimuthu.

'Marimuthu is a good name, isn't it? Deivanai had made a vow to the goddess Mariamma and so she wanted me to name the child Marimuthu,' he said.

Anjalai, who was also there, was distracted by Manikkam, who was working in the lower field. Manikkam was pruning the murungai trees, he too found his eyes seeking out Anjalai.

'Atha, I am going to our layyam, you come later,' said Anjalai and walked away.

Manikkam too prepared to follow her.

Manikkam was a well-mannered young man with a pleasant temperament. He was tall, broad-chested and witty. The very thought of him left Anjalai flustered.

Very soon, Anjalai and Manikkam were married in a simple ceremony. This marriage made a few things apparent to Valli. Poverty, she realised, was not a deterrent to love and longing. Sengamalai's need for Kaveri and Murugan's love for his wife testified this fact.

Sengamalai was indifferent and aloof, and acted like a stranger at his daughter Anjalai's wedding.

This annoyed Valli. Lakshmanan pretended not to notice anything and went about happily doing his work. He knew that his father was besieged by feelings of utter hopelessness and desperation. He saw the futility of his mother's anxiety regarding his father. Sengamalai had visibly aged, with wrinkled skin and graying hair. It was very apparent that Sengamalai had grown weary of his life. Valli too had lost her youthful vigour and was struggling with the onset of age. Of course, his brother Murugan was too busy with his new wife to notice these changes.

As soon as the wedding was over, Anjalai and Manikkam were taken to Murugan's layyam.

'The war is over, they say the sinna dorai will be returning soon,' said Lakshmanan.

'Yes, there was some talk about it in the field yesterday,' replied Murugan.

'Who cares? You think our life is going to change?'

'If the sinna dorai was here, these fellows will not be acting as they please?'

The next day, Manikkam and Anjalai started their new life at his parent's layyam. Manikkam's parents had recently come from India and were given a place in one of the newly constructed layyams.

'When the sinna dorai comes back I must ask him to give Anjalai her own room,' Valli thought to herself.

Anajalai's new life pleased Valli.

Manikkam was completely in love with Anjalai's youth and beauty. Her pleasant temperament made Manikkam a very happy man for a short while.

Sinna dorai returned from England. As soon as he returned, the periya dorai left for England, on a holiday. Three months after he had left, they received a message that he had taken ill and a replacement would be sent in his place. The sinna dorai took over the management of the plantation.

There were many changes on the plantations after the war. They were like blind people who had seen no light in their gloomy existence. But like a knotted thread, their lives unravelled. In the past, their belief in a faceless god kept them going. But now, they could feel the changes in the air, reinstating their belief in men and themselves. A beacon of hope was held out to them.

29

Sinna Dorai Maclean had been made the periya dorai. He had married while in England and was bringing back his wife. A young man named Allan McKinnon was sent to assist Maclean. He was lean and tall, with hawk-like eyes that were blood-shot all the time. The labourers instinctively felt they could not trust him and disliked him on sight. Within a few short months he earned their disapproval.

The periya kangany who had bought an estate nearby, stayed on at the plantation, having employed one of his relatives to take care of his estate. As he grew older he became more mellow and tolerant. He made his son-in-law his assistant and instructed him, in the presence of the labourers, 'These are all our workers, you have to take care of them.'

One day, a new motor vehicle arrived on the estate. It had been ordered from England for Maclean and he went to Colombo and drove it up to the estate. It made the same noise as the machines in the factory. The labourers were thrilled to see this new contraption and stared at it in wonder.

'What is this, sami?' someone asked the kangany.

'This is called the motor car. It is more convenient than riding a horse. At least that is what the dorai told me,' said the kangany.

'How does it work?' asked another.

'It runs on some kind of oil called petrol.'

When the motor car arrived, all of them gathered at the office, as if they were expecting a dignitary. They wanted to touch it, but they feared it was some kind of monster. They had never seen anything like it before.

The surprise lasted only for a few days, after which it wore off. The new source of excitement was the imminent arrival of Maclean's wife—the doraisani, from England. Maclean went to Colombo in his new car to bring her to the estate. They did not have to wait long before the dorai arrived with his wife. They were all dressed up in their finery – which was not much – and waited near the gate to welcome them.

The kangany had ordered two garlands from Kandy. He wore his Cannanore coat, Kollegal silk angavastram and looked resplendent with sandal paste and the kungumam adorning his forehead. He waited along with the sinna kangany, kanakapillais, the tea-maker and the clerks. They had a supercilious air about them, considering themselves superior to the labourers.

This was the first time that such an event was taking place in their plantation, which got them very excited.

'Don't crowd around like uncivilised savages. Behave yourselves,' the kangany reminded them again.

'Yes, what will the doraisani think of us! Behave yourselves,' ordered the kanakapillai.

Just then the sinna dorai, McKinnon, arrived on this horse. He got down and handed the reins to one of the men. Everyone became silent on seeing him. Only the kangany looked unintimidated.

In a short while, Maclean and his wife arrived in their motor car. The big gate was thrown open.

'Play the drums, play the music,' ordered the kangany, who had brought the musicians from Kandy.

'Both of you would be taken out in a procession to the bungalow,' said the kangany.

Maclean looked at his wife and said something. She looked unimpressed and whispered something back to him. Maclean turned to the kangany and told him, 'We will be going by car.'

'But please accept these garlands,' requested the kangany.

Both of them got down from the car and accepted the garlands. They shook hands with McKinnon and got back into the car. On reaching the bungalow, the workers were amazed at the trunks that were unloaded from the car. The children looked at the doraisani in wonder. Her very fair complexion and golden hair, left them awestruck.

The kangany tried to chase them away, 'Go away! Go away!' but they stubbornly stood there staring at Maclean's wife.

The couple went into the bungalow. The crowd slowly dispersed. The dorai came out again and thanked the kangany. Only Valli stayed behind.

'Atha, are you not coming to the layyam?' asked Murugan.

'You go, I will come in a while,' she replied.

After some time the dorai came out and found Valli waiting for him.

'What is it, Valli?' he asked her.

'Nothing, dorai,' she said, as she walked up to him and presented him with something she had unrolled from her sari. She bowed low and offered it to him with respect.

'What's this?' he asked, surprised.

'It's for your doraisani,' she said.

Maclean was moved by the gesture. He looked at the betel leaves and turmeric, that Valli had given him. He was surprised to find a silver coin glinting in its midst. He looked up and saw Valli with tears glistering in her eyes. He wondered how she managed to save this money, given her economic conditions. Unable to refuse such a noble gift, he thanked her. Valli walked away without a word.

࿊

Some important changes took place in the Rasikollai Rasa Estate and other plantations as well. In England, the price of tea dropped, with the management making noises about the loss. The company decided to cut down the workforce. They said they could not afford to pay them. The management in Rasikollai Rasa Estate wondered what to do. Bowing down to pressure from England, they laid off the older workers—Sengamalai was one among them. Valli was shocked.

Valli begged the dorai to give Sengamalai his job back. But he refused saying, 'He is a drunkard and hardly comes to work.' Valli's heart sank in despondency.

One day Anjalai complained to her, 'Atha, ayya takes my husband to the tavern. You better tell him not to. If I protest he picks up a fight with me. He is getting worse everyday.'

Valli was dismayed by her daughter's unhappiness. That evening she fought with Sengamalai.

'You have ruined your life, now why do you persist on ruining your daughter's life?' Valli raged at him.

'I didn't have to, he was already spoilt,' he replied.

'You are jobless, so you are using him to buy you drinks, I suppose.'

Sengamalai did not listen. He took Manikkam to the village often and got drunk. The dorais noticed their workers heading to the village regularly to drink, which increased theft. So, they decided to open a tavern in the estate itself.

'Muruga, did you hear the news?' Asked Lakshmanan one day while returning from work.

'What is it?'

'Some new labour office has been opened in the town. They have asked the management to wipe out all our old debts at the estate. Which means we do not have to pay off our debts to the Kanganys and Kanakapillais anymore. They have told them that they cannot hold on to those old debts.'

'Is it true?'

'Yes! I am just coming back from that office. Good times have begun for us,' said Lakshmanan.

'I don't know when that will be. By the way, do you know this fellow Manikkam is drinking and going around with that girl, Chittu?' asked Murugan.

'Yes, I heard about it. He needs to be beaten up, that will teach him a lesson,' said Lakshmanan.

'Don't do anything like that. It will be a disgrace for us! I will have a talk with him later. Will you come and have tea with us?'

'No, I have to go for a bath,' said Lakshmanan. On the way to the river he saw Chittu returning to her layyam after a bath. He decided to approach her.

'Chittu, why are you looking so dejected?'

'Nothing, I am fine,' Chittu answered him abruptly and tried to walk ahead.

'Hey, stop for a minute. Am I not smart enough for you, like Manikkam?' he asked her sarcastically.

'Chi! Shut up! What do you know about my machan?' she tried walking away from him again.

'Are you trying to run away? After his marriage, he belongs to another, do you know that? Why don't you call *me* your machan?' he baited her.

'Are you going to let me go or not?'

'What will you do if I don't? You will scream, I suppose?'

'Just let me go, will you?'

'Chittu, listen to me. Leave Manikkam alone, if you wish I will marry you. If you don't like me, I will get you married to anyone you like,' he appealed to her.

'Oh, my, my! Who do you think you are, offering to find a groom for me? What cheek!'

'You better do as I tell you, you don't know who I am! Be careful!' he warned menacingly before he let her go.

Chittu was furious. She complained about this to Manikkam who took up the issue with his wife Anjalai. He was related to Chittu, and his parents had expected him to marry her. But he had fallen in love with Anjalai and had disappointed them.

Anjalai and Manikkam had three children, and it was only after that, that they were given their own room. Their layyam was just a short distance away from Chittu's.

In a drunken rage Manikkam said, 'Who do you think your brother is? How dare he go to Chittu and talk all kinds of nonsense, wait and see what I'll do to him?'

'Why does it bother you so much when we talk about her? She not only ruins my family, now she's got you to speak for her! What kind of man are you?'

'The more I keep quiet, the sharper your tongue becomes, what do you think of yourself?' he sprang to get hold of her.

'Chi! You dare raise your hand against me? Try doing that, and I will beat you up with this log,' she threatened.

Meanwhile, they heard someone calling out for Manikkam. It was Chittu's mother, his aunt.

'I don't want any trouble for you because of us. If you had married Chittu, we wouldn't be having all this trouble. I am looking for a groom for her,' she said pathetically, as if she was sorry for the situation.

'Why athai, you don't have to cry because of this devil. Come,' he said and walked away with his aunt.

Anjalai was mad with rage. Suppressing the volcano that was spluttering inside her, she went straight to his aunt's layyam.

There she saw Chittu standing by the doorway in tears. Her mother and Manikkam were seated inside. Forgetting her reason for coming down there, she stood outside with a blank look on her face.

'What do you want?' asked Manikkam.

'I came to ask this shameless woman how she could live like this. She wants my husband and I think it's better to sit on the roadside and beg, rather than live like a dog,' said Anjalai and spat on the ground in contempt.

'Why are you behaving like a woman possessed. What do you care? I will go where I please, who are you to ask me?'

'If I can't ask you is *she* the one to ask you?'

'You are talking too much,' said Chittu, joining the fray. By then, the people from the layyam gathered around to watch the fun.

'Look at her! She has come to reason with me! Don't come with all that to me. Who the hell do you think you are, preaching to me?' Chittu continued bravely, sure of Manikkam's support.

'Who else can I talk to? You have stolen my husband,' said Anjalai.

'Will you go away from here or...' Manikkam came out menacingly, raising his hand.

By then someone had informed Murugan of the skirmish and he came rushing there with Lakshmanan.

'Anjalai, why did you come here? You better go to your layyam,' said Murugan annoyed with her.

'Oh, look, her brother has come to defend her,' said Manikkam with a sneer.

'Be careful, don't provoke me,' cautioned Murugan.

'Look at him, the big shot. He asks me not to provoke him.' Manikkam taunted him

'Why are you talking from in there, sitting inside like a woman? Why don't you come out here and talk?' said Lakshmanan.

'Oh! You have also come, have you?'

'Chi! You shameless fellow!'

'Anna, let us go. Let him go to hell! Let him go with that bitch!' said Anjalai to her brother, fearing the situation could get worse.

'That ass has no shame! First she ran around with that wet fowl Karuppan, then she went with Madasami, and now Manikkam, who knows who will be next? The whore!' said Lakshmanan.

'Keep quiet,' said Murugan trying to control the situation.

Manikkam was incensed. He pulled out the pruning knife that was secured to the roof and came running towards Lakshmanan in a frenzy.

'You want to chop me up? Go ahead, let us see!' Lakshmanan stood his ground, provoking Manikkam.

'Don't! Stop it!' The crowd tried to stop them. They locked into a fight and rolled on the ground. Manikkam held on to his pruning knife. Freeing himself for a moment he threw the pruning knife at Lakshmanan. Lakshmanan bent down in the nick of time. The pruning knife grazed his neck, and found its mark in Sockalingam who was standing behind him.

'Aiyo! Amma! Amma!' screamed Sockalingam and fell down like a felled tree.

Blood came gushing out of Sockalingam's neck. 'Take him to the hospital! Take him to the hospital!' they screamed. The relatives of the wounded man started beating up Manikkam.

Someone had informed the kangany and the kanakapillai about the fight and he came to the scene and stopped the crowd from mobbing Manikkam. Otherwise, they would have beaten him to death.

'Come, let us take Sockalingam to the hospital,' said Murugan. Two workers offered to carry him to the hospital. Someone's old vetti was used as bandage, but this did not staunch the flow of blood.

'We have to hand over Manikkam to the police!' said the kanakapillai.

'Yes, but how did this happen?' asked the kangany.

'Aiyo! Don't! Please don't! He was drunk and he did it unwittingly,' said Anjalai, pleading for mercy.

'I can do nothing. If Sockalingam lives, something can be done, otherwise it can be disastrous. The dorai will ask for Manikkam to be taken to the police,' said the kangany.

'All this happened because of you,' Anjalai accused, pointing to Chittu. She cried, pleaded, sobbed, begged, but to no avail.

Manikkam had sobered down. He stood frozen like a statue. They dragged him to the office.

Valli, hearing the news, came running.

'Come,' said Lakshmanan, as he tried to remove Anjalai from the scene. Blood was oozing down his neck.

'Lakshmana, what happened?' Valli asked anxiously.

'Come, let us go to our layyam. We can talk there,' Lakshmanan forced Anjalai to go with them.

30

'Muruga, how is Sockalingam?' asked Valli. Murugan had just returned from the hospital.

'The doctor says there is little chance of him surviving. His relatives have been asked to visit him,' said Murugan, his head held low. Valli felt as if someone had hammered a nail through her heart. Unable to support herself, she sat down. Her mouth felt dry and words would not come.

'They have taken Manikkam to the Kandy police station,' said Murugan, forcing the words out of his mouth.

Valli felt a shiver run through her spine.

'You have to inform Anjalai about this,' he said.

'You wretches! All of you got together and have destroyed my child's life! I am a sinner! You are asking me to go tell her?' She beat her head against the ground and wailed aloud.

'Athai, don't cry!' said Deivanai, trying to comfort Valli.

'You watch over her, I will go and see Anjalai!' said Deivanai, as she hastened to Anjalai's layyam.

Lakshmanan was there, waiting for some kind of news.

Anjalai, disheveled and distraught, was like a volcano, waiting to erupt.

'Go away! I don't need anyone! I am mourning the death of all my family today. Get lost all of you. Let me at least die in peace,' wailed Anjalai. However much Deivanai tried to calm her down, Anjalai remained agitated.

It soon got dark and misty. Deivanai lit a lamp to dispell the darkness. Anjalai's little children held on to Deivanai.

'The dorai wants you at the office!' said a messenger.

Anjalai, Murugan and Lakshmanan went to the office. It took a long time for them to get back home.

☙

'He has died.' Those few words tore through the darkness of the night piercing her heart.

'Who is dead?' Valli asked, for a moment forgetting their circumstances. As soon as realisation set in, their sleep vanished.

Anjalai held on to the doorway and slid down. 'Go bring some water, Deivanai!' said Murugan. They tried to revive Anjalai. As soon as she gained consciousness she looked at everyone like a woman gone mad. Everyone seemed like monsters to her, huge and threatening.

'Go away! I need no one here! Go away! Mind your own business, go!' cried Anjalai burying her face between her hands. They could not comfort her. At last, tired and worn out, she fell asleep, momentarily forgetting her troubles.

As the days flew past, Anjalai refused to have anything to do with her family. She refused even to look at them.

The case was held at Kandy. Anjalai, Murugan and Lakshmanan were summoned as witnesses. That was the first time that Anjalai had ever set foot outside the plantation. Unfortunately for her, she was in no state to appreciate or dislike the experience. Prison life had completely transformed Manikkam. Anjalai was pained by his appearance. He had lost weight and was unshaven. His eyes were bleak like they had lost all hope. She sobbed, rueing her fate and berating the god who did this to her.

The handcuffs weighed heavy on Manikkam's hands. Everytime he moved his hands they clanged noisily, making Anjalai cringe.

As soon as he saw Anjalai, his eyes filled with tears. Chittu was also called in to testify. She had come with her parents. She did not appear to have any concern for Manikkam's plight.

The woman for whom Manikkam had given up his self-respect, dignity and honour, was now spurning him. Manikkam felt that he should have murdered her along with Sockalingam. Chittu was aware of Manikkam's rage. She stood stiff, avoiding his eyes. Murugan and Lakshmanan noticed these undercurrents. Murugan was stricken by conflicting emotions of anger and pity.

Lakshmanan looked like he had arrived at a resolution, and he seemed to be smirking at Chittu.

The case was soon closed. Since Sockalingam had died, they charged Manikkam with murder and sentenced him to be hanged.

31

'It is two days since ayya had gone to the village, he hasn't returned as yet,' said Murugan softly.

'Yes, what does he care. Last week he fought with me and took away all my wages. He's got to spend it all on his drink before he gets back,' said Valli, chewing betel leaves.

'Now we have a toddy tavern on the estate itself,' said Murugan, stacking the firewood.

'They have laid him off from work. Having worked for all these years I thought they might give him something! I asked the dorai and he said there was nothing to give. What do I do?' Valli said in a voice filled with despondency.

'Are they the people to give you anything for free? They ask us to bury our dead under the tea bushes to save money on fertilisers!'

'Nothing seems to work for us. That girl Anjalai won't let any one come near her. Thinking of her makes my heart heavy. I never dreamt that at such a young age her life will come to this. If only I had known, I would have given her in marriage to someone far away—like Meenakshi. At least I don't have to see her suffering everyday,' said Valli sorrowfully.

'You're right, but what can we do now? I even offered her part of my wages but she firmly refuses to accept. That fellow Lakshmanan is loafing here and there. From next week onwards the dorai said that they will pay our wages at the office. It seems the government has brought a new law to that effect,' said Murugan.

'What is the use? Nothing great is going to come of it. They say the tea prices have gone down and have laid off more workers. These people are now roaming the streets.'

'They are not just roaming the streets, they are begging on the streets. They are unable to even return home to India. The past few year have been difficult ones.'

'Athai, have some hot tea,' Deivanai called out from inside.

'Hmm, like that is all I need. Has Thailammai returned from the river? That fellow Lakshmanan is playing the fool not giving me a paise from his wages.'

'Oh yes, I must give you what I earn too. Then your husband will have a good time drinking, I suppose,' said Lakshmanan, who had just come in.

'Alright, alright! Watch your tongue and talk with care,' said Valli, irritated.

'I'll do that, but you try to stop the world from wagging its tongue. They are laughing at my father, saying he begs on the streets for money! Enough! After all these years of work he's been reduced to a beggar now,' said Lakshmanan outraged.

'What did you say? He's begging? Who said so? Are you mad?'

'I am not joking. If you have no way of earning a living what else can you do? After working for all these years, if you are kicked out in your old age with nothing, you have no choice but to beg for your food. After the lay off do you know how many workers are on the streets? Go and see for yourself if you don't believe me,' said Lakshmanan.

'Go tell this to someone else! As long as I live I won't let anyone from my house beg!'

'That's right! What you earn is not enough for your upkeep! How are you going to support the rest of us? Alright, I am going to the village before it gets dark. I am thinking of taking the vegetables from our garden to the fair this Sunday.'

'What are you going to do with the money?'

'I will do something!'

'Take the brinjals from my garden. There is a good yield this time,' said Murugan.

'Eat something before you go,' said Deivanai, with concern.

'I don't want anything. I am going with Pachamuthu to watch the Kaman kuthu,' said Lakshmanan as he hurried to meet his friend.

Valli was disturbed by Lakshmanan's words. She felt rage and tears threatening to overwhelm her. The fact that someone from her family should stoop to begging, made her cringe with shame.

32

Time and circumstances brought changes not only to Rasikollai Rasa Estate, but also to the rest of the country.

Under the government's new regulations every plantation was ordered to build a school and establish a well-equipped hospital. Moreover, the Indian government decided to stop the influx of workers going to Ceylon. These policies brought some good and bad changes to the plantation.

One of the welcome changes was that all their old debts were wiped out for good. The workers felt relieved of a heavy burden weighing their minds. Their troubled souls now felt a surge of energy and enthusiasm.

'At least now we will get our wages every month,' said Murugan. His last child was hanging on to his shoulders, there was a note of peace in his voice.

'Yes, but debtors will arrive in new forms,' said Lakshmanan, with a sneer in his voice.

'Whatever maybe the reforms, it will all be the same to us,' said Valli.

'Yes, a wolf cannot become a cat,' Lakshmanan reiterated.

'Alright! Now go and look for your good-for-nothing father and find out what he is up to,' said Valli.

'Where do I go looking for him? He must be sitting somewhere and begging. In a short while you too will come to that state. That's all you get for working on this estate,' said Lakshmanan, hoeing the garden.

'What's the matter with you? You have become too cynical. Instead of having given birth to you, I wish I had given birth to a stone!' said Valli bitterly.

'That would have saved both of us a lot of trouble.'

'Muruga, why don't you send Marimuthu to the new school on the estate?' said Valli.

'Yes, I must do that. There was a teacher who joined last week, but he has already left saying he does not like the estate. They say there is a new teacher coming next week. I must do something then.'

'He should at least know how to read and write a letter. Nowadays the world is different.

'You think education is going to help him become a big shot?' asked Lakshmanan sarcastically.

'Even if nothing like that happens, as atha says, it will be useful to know how to read and write,' said Murugan in defense of his mother.

'If our children study, our lives could become better,' said Deivanai, who had been silent so far.

'First let them establish the school,' said the ever cynical Lakshmanan, as he rose to wash his hands.

'Valli! Valli!' they heard some one call.

'Who is it?'

'It is me, Kaveri. Are you here? I heard your daughter Anjalai is very sick. I had to let you know. Go and see her. There's no one to feed the children, they look hungry and starved. Poor things,' said Kaveri.

'How long has it been this way?' asked Valli.

'Must be about four or five days.'

'That is why I did not see her at the field. I wanted to ask yesterday, but somehow forgot about it. She does not want to listen to us,' Valli said in frustration.

'It's getting late, I'll see you later,' said Kaveri.

'Wait, have some tea before you go.'

'No, just give me a betel leaf if you have some.'

'Well, the tea is ready, have some. Deivanai bring some hot tea. Ask Thailammai to take care of the house. I'll just go and check on Anjalai, I might stay with her tonight,' said Valli as she started out.

'Wait, I will also come with you to the layyam,' said Kaveri.

Valli saw Anjalai's children playing by their doorway, naked, dirty and unwashed. They did not notice her in the dark. Valli was dismayed to find them in this state.

'Where is your mother?' she asked, as she walked in.

'Paati, you have come, have you?' Anjalai's daughter Kamalam ran towards her and hugged her.

'Amma, paati has come! Paati has come.' The other two ran inside, announcing her arrival with glee.

'Anjalai, since I had not seen you at work these past few days I asked the kankapillai today about you. He said you were ill so I have come to see you,' said Valli. She removed Anjalai's blanket and touched her forehead, she found that she was burning with fever.

'What is it, is it malaria?' she asked. Anjalai moaned softly and turned towards the wall without a word. Valli covered her with a blanket and turned to survey the room. There were only ashes in the hearth. She wondered for how many days it had remained unlit. She went to the neighbour's room and borrowed some matches and lit the fire. She also found out that the children had had no food all these days.

'Kamalam, wear this dress will you! Come here, you fellows,' she called out to the children. She bathed them with hot water and put some fresh clothing on them. Anjalai's attitude made her fear for her. Her mind was in a turmoil.

Valli made some food for the children and put them to sleep. She then gave some kanji to Anjalai.

'I don't want anything! Go away,' she pushed her mother away.

'Don't eat for my sake, eat for the sake of your children.' Valli said, trying to comfort her.

33

Even after Anjalai had recovered from her illness, she did not normalise her relationship with her mother. Valli would go to Anjalai's layyam, take care of the children, feed them and return. Anjalai allowed this, as she fell ill quite often and the children too looked forward to being with their grandmother.

'We have arranged for Thailammai's wedding next month. Our Chidambaram is the groom,' Valli told Anjalai.

'How does Thailammai feel about this?' asked Anjalai.

'She has no objection.'

'Hmm... Where is ayya? Does he come home or is he staying in the village?'

'He comes when he needs something. It seems he is begging on the streets and people are talking about us.'

'What can be done about that? There is no work on the estate, no wages. At his age no one will give him any work. Let it be, he too needs something.'

'Is begging a solution? Why can't he stay put at home and eat whatever we have, even if it is just kanji.'

'We cannot reform him now. There are so many like him who have come to the state of begging, do you know that?'

'Let's not talk about him. Whatever god has in store for us, let it be.'

'Amma, they have called for you at the kangany's house,' said Kamalam to her mother Anjalai.

'Anjalai, we can see the kangany's new house from here. Is the kanakapillai's house also down that valley?'

'Yes, now that he has moved into this new house, I go and help them with the housework. That woman gives these children food, if she has any leftovers,' said Anjalai with a note of resentment. Noticing a strangeness in her speech Valli turned and looked at Anjalai. It was clear that there was something troubling Anjalai.

'Must you work in their house?' she asked softly.

'How else do I run my family? I am alone now. Anyway, I'll soon be back from the kangany's house,' said Anjalai hurrying down the slope, as if she did not wish to discuss the matter anymore.

Valli stood at the doorway watching the evening sun shed its soft rays on the roofs of the village houses and the green rice fields. This picture took her back to her village, Senthur. If only there had been such green fields in her homeland, then they would never have had to leave their village and come to this alien land. Thinking again of Anjalai's life she felt as if someone had set fire to her heart.

'Atha, atha! Ayya is back and he is throwing out the things in our room,' Thailammai came rushing towards Valli.

'You look after these children, I will go to our layyam.'

'I informed anna before I came to you.'

'Good, now cook some rice, I'll return soon,' said Valli, as she hurried home.

After flinging their few possessions about the room, Sengamalai was sitting on the doorstep exhausted. Murugan was trying to calm him down.

'What is this ayya? What do we do if you cause such trouble? What can atha do?' said Murugan.

'Let her go to hell, who cares? There is no difference between living and dying. What do we have left after having sold our bodies and souls to these fellows?'

'What is the use in flinging our things around? How is it going to help?'

'I want money now! She must have hidden it somewhere!' said Sengamalai. Valli heard him, on arriving at the scene.

'Yes, I have kept it aside for your funeral!' said Valli angrily.

'Unfortunately I am not dead as yet. Only if you give me some money I'll let you be. Otherwise…'

'Otherwise, what will you do?'

'You will know that soon.'

'You've been sent to make my life miserable.'

'Here take this,' Murugan took out a few coins and gave it to his father.

'Why are you giving him money?' asked Lakshmanan, who had just come home.

'Why should that bother you?' asked Sengamalai.

'Why? You take our money for your drinks and then go around begging! We are ashamed to call you our father—because of you people laugh at us.'

'Who do you think you are? Get lost,' Sengamalai threw a towel over his shoulder, set right his vetti and got ready to leave. Tears poured down Valli's cheeks. There was a kind of yearning as she looked at Sengamalai. He did not notice her. Like a mad man, he kept counting the coins, over and over again. He secured them in the corner of his vetti, tucking the parcel into his waist.

'Valli, give me some betel leaves,' he asked his wife. She took her betel pouch from her waist and gave it to him. 'Whatever happens, I hope you do not come to the state of begging like me,' having said that, he walked away from his family without looking back.

They watched him go and did not speak a word until he disappeared into the distance.

34

It had rained all morning. 'The rain has just let up, I am going to fetch some water,' said Valli. Anjalai was ill and had once again taken to bed.

'I am taking the children with me. They can bring the firewood,' Valli said again. Anjalai did not speak, the place just echoed with her coughing.

'I have left some hot tea for you, drink it when you want,' instructed Valli as she stepped out.

'Kamalam, come here. Where are Ganesan and Muniyan?'

'They are playing over there,' Kamalam pointed her finger to show where her brothers were playing. The child was about eight and was unkempt and dirty. But in her eyes one could see mischief and enthusiasm.

'Paati, shall I also bring a pot to fetch water?' asked Kamalam.

'No, it is difficult to walk in this slush. You can carry some firewood if we find any in the river,' said Valli.

The two boys who were playing in the puddle, also went along with her.

'Dei! Walk carefully, the path is slushy,' Valli warned them repeatedly.

Periya dorai Maclean was walking towards his bungalow down that pathway.

'Valli, where are you going in this rain?' he asked.

'I am going to fetch some water, dorai,' she replied.

He noticed that Valli had passed her prime. The grey streaks were prominent. Instead of her upright stance and purposeful walk, she had begun to stoop, and there was a somber look about her.

'How many years has it been since you came to this estate, Valli?' This sudden question from him surprised her.

'I don't know anything about counting the years, dorai. I have been here since I got married. They say my husband was born on this estate. Now I have my own grandsons and granddaughters,' she replied.

'When I first saw you, you were a little girl. Now you have become an old woman,' he said with amusement.

'Yes dorai, I am an old woman now,' she agreed.

'But you are still a good worker. The young girls on the estate are not as good as you in picking tea,' he said quickly, as though to pacify her.

'As long as I have life in my body I can work, my hands will not fail me.'

'Alright, get back before there's another spell of rain. Are these Anjalai's children?'

'Yes, dorai!'

'Is Sengamalai still drinking a lot?'

'Yes, he is becoming too troublesome.'

'Why is Lakshmanan being troublesome? What's the matter?'

'What can I do? He does not listen to anyone, dorai.'

'Alright, let's see, you know I have kept him on because of you,' said the dorai and walked away towards the bungalow.

Valli stood there for a moment looking at his receding figure—her thoughts were broken by Kamalam calling out to her.

'Paati, these two are fighting, come quickly.'

'Dei! Stop fighting, don't be naughty,' Valli hurried along, shouting after them. 'Why are you fighting?'

'Look paati, he took away the sweet you gave me.'

She smacked the older boy Ganesan and dragged him along. The younger one followed, crying all the way.

As she washed the dirty clothes in the river she looked around. How many thousand times must she have washed and bathed in this river?

The children were running around picking firewood and stacking them on the bank. On the other side of the river, Valli could hear the farmers singing as they worked in their fields. The music floated in the air. Instead of putting her at ease there was something in the air that bothered her. The water in the river was gushing like a screaming demon. She was momentarily lost in her thoughts and did not hear Kamalam calling out to her urgently. 'Paati, water! Water!' She finally heard the shouts and turned to see what the commotion was all about.

She saw Ganesan standing on a boulder in the middle of the river. Kamalam and Muniyan ran towards her.

She saw the water rushing down in a flood and coming towards them. She realised that there was no time for her to rescue the boy.

'Run, run and come to me,' she shouted out to him.

'I will come as soon as the water goes down,' he shouted back.

'No, come now, run!' she shouted agitatedly. A huge sheet of water rolled down the slope. She knew that the hapless child would not be able to withstand the force of the flood.

'Kamalam, both of you stand on the shore, I will go get Ganesan!' Before she could finish saying these words, she saw that the water had already reached them. She saw the little child looking at the big wave coming towards him like a monster. He was still holding the pieces of firewood he had picked in his hands. The water engulfed him and in a second he was washed off the boulder like a fallen leaf in the wind.

'Ganesa, Ganesa!' She ran along the banks of the river calling out to the child. She saw his flailing hands put up a brave fight. The ruthless water prevailed.

Valli saw the child pushed towards the bank, she stretched her hand to catch hold of him. But she slipped and fell and saw the child getting irrevocably lost in the flood. A few people rushed to rescue her, carrying her to safer ground. Otherwise, Valli too would have lost her life that day.

Beating her chest, and sobbing aloud, she ran to Anjalai's layyam. By then Kamalam and Muniyan had gone home and given the terrible news to their mother.

Anjalai was standing near the doorway like a statue. Valli beating her chest lamented in pain.

'I am a sinner, I am a sinner! I killed that child!' Valli wailed, grief-stricken. Valli's sorrow deeply affected the onlookers, who felt their hearts weighed down by this news.

'What can you do? That was his fate!' People tried to console her.

Anjalai stood still, rooted to the doorway.

People were amazed by her reaction. They wondered if Anjalai was a heartless woman with no feelings.

Valli rolled on the ground, sobbing in grief. While the people commiserated with Valli, they just ignored Anjalai. Finally, like a dam breaching its walls, Anjalai gave in to the uncontainable anguish that beset her. She covered her face with her hands and sobbed inconsolably.

'My child! My child, born in this sinner's womb! What does it matter whether it lived or died, it is all the same! I couldn't feed the child one decent meal, that is why god has taken that child away from me! I am a sinner… I am a sinner…' She beat her head against the wall, and howled in grief.

Someone in that layyam lit a tin lamp which flickered in the wind and died out. It was lit again and kept in a protected corner. The rain poured steadily and dripped through the leaky roof. Water collected in small pools on the uneven floor.

People who were searching for the child along the riverbank returned empty-handed. They could not find the child, it had grown dark. They promised to continue the search in the morning.

Anjalai sat in a corner and wept through the night. Valli was like a demented woman, howling in pain.

The children were caught between them, they sat in a corner, frightened, watching their elders' lamentations.

Murugan hurried to his sister's layyam braving the rain, to offer his support.

The next morning, it stopped raining. There was an eerie silence—uprooted trees and fallen branches stood testimony to the storm on the previous day.

The flood had subsided in the river. People searched along the shore and found the body of the child buried in a heap of rubbish. He was still holding on to a twig he had collected. The child looked as if he was blissfully asleep.

35

Valli sat on the doorstep chewing betel leaves and staring at the stars embedded in the sky. Clouds floated across the skies, the silver rays of the moon sneaked through the trees, spreading their light.

Valli heard the voices of the periya kangany and her son Murugan on the pathway.

'In the month of Aadi I am planning to go to Kadirgamam, to take part in the festival,' said Murugan.

'What Muruga, why have you suddenly decided to go to Kadirgamam?'

'Ayya, about ten to twenty families from the estate have decided to go on this pilgrimage.'

'Hmm, let's see! I must ask the dorai about it, I will ask him tomorrow,' said the kangany.

'Alright ayya,' said Murugan as he took leave. He proceeded to Valli's layyam and called out to her.

'Atha, what are you doing, seated in the dark?' he asked.

'I just sat down to chew some betel leaves. Come, sit.'

'Where is Lakshmanan?'

'Who knows?'

'I told our kangany that I wish to go to Kadirgamam, would you like to come too? Everyone says it is a very holy place! The kangany says he is going to build a temple on the estate this year. He is also planning a Mariatha poosai next Chithirai.'

'Let's see, I too have been wanting to see that god Murugan in Kadirgamam before I die. Having worked all my life what am I going to take with me?'

'Well, let us all go! What is this I hear that Lakshmanan is roaming around the town gathering people? The kangany ayya was talking to me about it.'

'Men? For what?' she asked, not understanding Murugan.

'In Hatton, a man has founded an Indian organization to help those who have been laid off from the plantations. I think he is involved with these people.'

'I don't understand these things.'

'They have formed a union to help those who have been laid off, to return to India. He takes the government's help to do this.'

'Is that so? What has Lakshmanan to do with it?'

'Lakshmanan, unable to stay quiet, is recruiting men for the organisation. Mad fellow! Instead of minding his own business, he is flinging mud on his own head like a rutting elephant.'

'Let us ask him about this when he comes back. If this news reaches the dorai's ears, we are done for.'

'What kind of madness is this,' grumbled Murugan.

'It is all my fate! What can I do? Is that fellow Mari studying well? How is Papathi?' she asked after her grandchildren.

'Mari wishes to go to the school in town, but with our pay how is that possible?'

'What's wrong with the plantation school?'

'Don't ask. In the plantation school there is only one teacher for all the classes and he doesn't teach them properly. He asks them to fetch water, tend to his vegetable garden, bring firewood...Mari refuses to do all this and insists he wants to go to the town school. My father-in-law also thinks this is a good idea.'

'In that case why don't you send him to the town school?'

'I must do something about it this month.'

Just as they were talking, Lakshmanan arrived.

'What is the talk all about?' Lakshmanan asked.

'It's all about you! They say you are roaming around as you please? Don't associate yourself with those people! If the word reaches the dorai's ears, there will be trouble.'

'What do you know about it? Don't talk like you understand these things,' said Lakshmanan in an irritated voice.

'I don't have to know anything! If you stay quiet that is enough, understand?' she said.

'Why, what's the problem?'

'Your activities have already come to the notice of the kangangy. If the dorai also comes to know about it you will lose your job,' said Valli.

'Those days are over, where you fear their threats. Ask them to mind their own business,' said Lakshmanan.

'Thailammai, serve me food. I need to go out soon,' Lakshmanan called out to his sister, as he sat down to eat.

'Alright! I will see you later. The one who does not obey at home will be made to obey outside the house,' said Murugan, quoting a popular saying.

Valli sighed and said, 'I just hope you don't jeopardise your job!'

Lakshmanan, without bothering to reply, ate hurriedly and left.

'Atha, have your dinner and go to sleep,' called out Thailammai. Valli was lost in her own thoughts.

A few weeks after this incident, the dorai sent word for Lakshmanan.

Valli, not feeling too well, had stayed back home. Hearing the summons for her son, she grew apprehensive. Lakhmanan had finished work early that day and returned home.

'What will happen now, Lakshmana?' Valli asked her son fearfully.

'Who knows? We are are all slaves over here, aren't we? We've got to go running when the summons come,' said Lakshmanan sarcastically and made his way to the office.

Lakshmanan looked confident and motivated as he made his way to the office. Valli often looked at him admiringly and felt proud of her son. But she was also baffled by his unfamiliar modern ways which made her uncomfortable.

Lakshmanan felt in his heart that difficult times were ahead and he had no other alternative but to face it. Would he have to be a slave all his life? Generation after generation they have lived this life of slavery. Will they ever know freedom? However much they toil, would any boss dare to give them what is legitimately theirs? They will only want to make more and more profit to live a life of luxury. The workers were used as machines. These thoughts filled his heart with rage, and a fierce force drove him towards an unknown future.

Yes, there was a person, in the big city, fighting for the labourers. He knew he was a part of his organisation. Why should the dorais be worried about that? Is this organisation going to affect them? How? Why? If we ask for fair play, is it wrong? Is it a crime?

He reached the office with all these thoughts flitting through his mind.

Periya Dorai Maclean, the periya kangany and the kanakapillai had gathered there and were discussing among themselves. He felt revulsion and fear grip him.

'Come Lakshmana,' periya dorai called him in.

'You had sent word for me?'

'Yes, something very important has come up,' began the periya kangany.

Lakshmanan stood there silent. The kangany looked him up and down, noticing his modern haircut, immaculately white vetti and shirt.

'It seems you are recruiting men for some union, is it true?' asked the kangany in a casual way.

'No ayya!' he replied.

'We have proof,' said the dorai.

'Yes, we have plenty of proof,' said the kanakapillai. Just then a labourer called Maruthai, who worked with Lakshmanan, entered the room. Lakshmanan wondered what he was doing over there.

'Maruthai, did Lakshmanan say anything about a union? Has he been recruiting labourers?'

'Yes ayya. I saw him having discussions with Pitchamuthu, Sivasamy and others about a union. They wanted me to join them, but I refused. I cannot betray the hand that feeds me,' he said sanctimoniously.

'What do you have to say to this?' asked the kangany.

'Lakshmanan should not stay on the estate any more,' said the kanakapillai.

'You have to leave the estate by tomorrow, you understand? If we let you be, the others too would soon be corrupted!' said the dorai.

'What crime have I committed? Why must I leave the estate? asked Lakshmanan.

'You can't do anything worse than this. Come settle your accounts tomorrow and leave the estate. Be happy that we haven't taken you to task,' said the kanakapillai. The dorai watched the proceedings without saying a word.

The sudden decision stunned Lakshmanan. What was he going to do without a job and no place to go? 'I have not done anything to deserve a dismissal? If you are unhappy with my work, tell me about it,' said Lakshmanan.

'Do we have to elaborate on the reason? By dawn you must leave this estate. We must not see your face over here anymore, understand?' said the kangany. He stroked his graying whiskers with his fingers and glared at him as if he would burn him alive.

Lakshmanan knew that there was no point in trying to make them see reason. He stared at the merciless faces of the people in the office. What truly bothered him was the betrayal of a fellow worker. He found it very puzzling that the very people he was trying to help could be so treacherous and cowardly.

Distracted with his own thoughts he walked towards his layyam. It was still drizzling.

He wondered how he would break this news to his mother. He considered leaving the plantation without informing anyone. He felt disgraced and ashamed about the whole thing.

He felt there was nothing more shameful than being dismissed for no culpable offence. But the entire episode served to strengthen his resolution and reaffirm his beliefs. There was a need for a revolution and he was ready for the struggle.

He reached the layyam and found Valli waiting anxiously for his return. She was picking lice from Thailammai's head.

'Why did the Dorai ask you to come?'

'Oh that, hmm...'

'You look dejected. What happened?'

'Nothing, it's just that by tomorrow morning I must leave this estate. They have dismissed me.'

'Does that mean you have no work here anymore? Our family has been here for so many years, and now suddenly they are asking you to leave? What crime have you committed that they should come to this decision?' she asked choking with emotion.

Her stomach churned. Was this the first sign of the changes taking place on the plantation?

Thinking of their slavish lives, with no voice or rights, enraged her.

'Tomorrow I will go ask the dorai for an explanation. Otherwise, I will also stop working,' declared Valli, as tears gushed out in anger.

Lakshmanan felt like laughing, and could not suppress his amusement.

'What are you laughing at?'

'Nothing, I am just laughing at what you said. Asking the dorai is not going to help anyone...! If *you* don't go to work, you think they can't find someone else? They will find someone else alright! You will be reduced to begging on the streets like ayya. *They* are not going to lose anything! You think you can't be replaced?' he asked sarcastically.

Valli realised the truth in what he said. But her heart refused to accept this truth.

'After working for so many years you think they will dismiss me just like that? What kind of reasoning is this? Is this fair?' she asked trying to reassure herself. But her own words sounded hollow and empty even to her.

'I think I should leave now,' said Lakshmanan.

'Where will you go in this rain and chill? Stay, tomorrow we will once again talk about this to them. How can they dismiss you so suddenly. Is there no one to question them?'

'What more is there to discuss? Even Murugan's father-in-law, the kanakapillai did not speak up for me. Do we need anyone else? Anyway, I will soon put an end to all this.' He gathered together his few belongings, two or three vettis and shirts, a few prized possessions and a photograph of Mahatma Gandhi.

'Why don't you leave in the morning? Why do you have to leave in this rain?' asked Valli, still not able to come to terms with this sudden turn of events.

'Rain or shine, everything is the same to me now. Have we not worked in the pouring rain? It is nothing new for us,' he said and took his bundle, ready to leave.

Valli, not willing to stop him after that, had become silent. Her heart was filled with resentment. It was not easy letting go of her son, whether he be a criminal or a saint. She tried to ease the terrible pain that was lodged in her heart.

Lakshmanan was at a loss for words. He wondered if he would ever be able to see his mother again. His sister Thailammai and brother Kumaran shivered in a corner knowing that something awful had happened and that nothing could be done about it.

With nothing more to say, Lakshmanan left in that pouring rain. His figure was soon swallowed by the dark night.

36

That year, the month of Aadi brought a new experience to Valli's life. From the time she had come to live on the estate she had never left the plantation, excepting for the one time she was permitted to visit her mother's home.

She had heard about trains, but she had never seen one. That year, the journey to Kathirgamam gave them something to look forward to.

They waited at the railway station at Nawalapitiya to board the train. Valli, along with Murugan's family and forty other workers from the same estate, were on their way to Kathirgamam.

There was quite a crowd waiting at the station to go to Kathirgamam. They were all calling out, 'Arohara, arohara! Muruga! Muruga!'

Kathirgamam had a temple for Murugan. The god was supposed to have come to Lanka to marry the hunter's daughter, Valli; and after the marriage, he had lived on in Kathirgamam. Every year, the temple was opened in the month of Aadi, when they celebrated the marriage of Valli and Murugan. The festival lasted for fifteen days, after which the temple was closed till the following year. People from all over the country walked many miles by foot to visit this temple.

Valli, looking at the crowd of people surging around her, was reminded of her trip from India with her parents, when she was a little girl. Their frenzied cries of 'Arohara!' made her feel rejuvenated.

The train pulled at last into the station with a roar. As it ground to a halt, the crowds surged into the train, pushing and pulling, edging their way into the third class compartments.

'Muruga, have you got all the things? Check again, Deivanai do not stand near the door! Bring the children and come inside!' Valli kept instructing her family. The fear that the train might derail, unable to carry the weight of so many passengers, made her sweat with fright.

'Mari, don't put your head out of the window!' she dragged him inside.

They reached Haputale, crushed and jostled by the crowd. Deivanai's baby cried the entire time, oppressed by the crowd.

From Haputale, they had to take a bus to Tissamaharama. It was extremely cold and their fingers and legs felt frozen. The next day, they left for Tissamaharama, from where they had to walk for thirteen miles to reach Kathirgamam. By then, they were tired, exhausted and weary, without proper food and water. Since they were used to climbing the hills on the estate, they plodded on, carrying their children on their shoulders and walking with unfaltering faith in the god Murugan, calling out 'Arohara!' all the way.

They had to walk through the jungles, in a forest trail. But neither the dense jungles or the wild animals frightened them. They chose to walk after the sun had gone down, to avoid the blazing heat of the day.

The next morning, they reached the river Menik Ganga which ran close to the temple. The crystal clear waters of the river revived them and they hurried to pay homage to the god, crying out 'Arohara! Arohara!' as they made their way to the temple.

Valli too was influenced by the magical atmosphere. There were no priests in the temple; two Sinhala men wearing lungis, with betel juice dribbling from the corners of their mouth, were accepting their coconuts for the poosai.

Valli expected to see a statue of Murugan as she entered the temple. Instead, she only saw a curtain painted with the figures of Murugan and his two wives, Valli and Deivanai. There was a smile on Murugan's face as he appeared seated on his peacock.

'Can't we go in any further?' asked Valli.

'No, you have to stay here. The poosari will offer the coconuts and bring it back to us.'

Just then the bells began to ring and the drums began to beat—two men with their mouths covered with a piece of cloth came carrying a kavadi in which there was a pot of rice. Behind them were young women carrying lamps. Everyone was surprised to see that the women only wore a piece of cloth around their waist and nothing more.

The women sang a ritual song. As soon as they finished they left. People said that these women and men were from the hunter community, and that their women were the maids to the god's consort, Valli.

Valli was transfixed by the ceremony. The lord who chose his bride from the hunter community was offered rice, venison, honey and millet. Valli felt spiritually recharged and was curious to know what was behind the curtain.

The only thing she could do was pray to the god Murugan to take care of her family and give them his blessings.

She prayed for her husband, Sengamalai, and her son, Lakshmanan. She wondered where they were, and what they were doing.

37

'Atha, Anjalai wants you to visit her!' said Thailammai, Valli's youngest daughter, standing by the doorway. She removed her basket and hung the sack that covered her head on the clothesline.

'What for?' asked Valli, as she cleaned the rice.

'She said something about not being well. I am going to the river for a bath,' said Thailammai and rushed off towards the river.

The kangany's son Shanmugam, who was walking by, paused to watch Thailammai. He found her immensely attractive. Valli noticed his gaze. 'I need to get Thailammai married quickly,' she thought as she walked to Anjalai's room.

'What is it Anjalai? I heard you wanted to see me?'

Anjalai was blowing the fire and the room was filled with smoke.

'This firewood is damp and does not burn at all. My eyes hurt with all the smoke,' said Anjalai, rubbing her eyes as she stepped out.

'Kamalam! Put the firewood near the fire to dry!' she called out to her daughter.

'Thailammai said you were not feeling well. What's the matter?'

'Nothing in particular. I feel a little…'

Valli stared at her face, puzzled. She went up to the cooking area. Usually she would find nothing there, sometimes not even rice. Anjalai and her three children had to live on the meagre wages she was paid. Valli, of course, tried to help her as much as possible.

But on that day there was plenty of food—an unexplainable riddle to Valli.

'Anjalai, did you borrow money from the kangany?' Valli quietly asked her daughter.

'No,' she said uneasily, standing near the doorway and looking outside. In that dim twilight, Anjalai's appearance and talk disturbed Valli.

'Anjalai, I've been asking you questions and you don't give me straight answers,' said Valli. Anjalai turned around and Valli saw her fully for the first time that evening. The difference in her appearance made Valli incredulous with surprise. She felt faint, as if the whole world was crumbling around her. For a moment she felt her throat constrict, words failed her. She staggered and held on to the wall.

'How many months?' she asked softly.

'Six,' said Anjalai. Her face was red with shame and sorrow.

Valli felt weighed down by the scandal, disgrace and humiliation lying await for them. The moment society witnesses a person's deviation from societal mores, it will immediately ostracise the person and will not stop short of besmirching the person's reputation. This is a well-known truth, and the workers on the estate were no different.

'Who is it?' asked Valli.

'Sinna dorai,' she answered. A film of tears shone in her eyes.

Was it only hunger and need to feed her children that had made Anjalai sell herself? Or was she raped by the demons on the estate, because she could not escape from their clutches? What will the world say? A woman without a husband, now pregnant—how was this to be explained? It was nothing new on the estate. Everyone knew that the kangany's wife visited the sinna dorai's bungalow during the day. Many have seen her. The kangany also went around chasing women workers on the estate by night.

The past was done and over. Valli had to concern herself with the future.

'Why don't you marry someone?' said Valli.

'Marriage? After all this? As if I have not suffered enough!' Anjalai answered with revulsion and disgust.

Scattered thoughts danced like devils in Valli's mind.

The silence of the dark room was interrupted only by the damp logs crackling in the cooking fire. Valli's situation did not permit her to take care of Anjalai or protect her. She blamed herself for whatever had happened.

Anjalai's thoughts raced back to that fateful day. While she was picking tea, the sinna dorai had come from behind and said, 'Put your basket down!' She had obeyed wordlessly, her head held down. His soft fleshy hands had caught her calloused, work-roughened hands and pulled her down to the ground under the bushes. His lust-filled eyes had burnt her and she had shivered with fear. His flaming red hair was ruffled by the wind. He was sweating with the urgency of his desire and finally gave in to its dictate.

He was probably reminded of his days in England where they hunted with packs of hounds. Here, the hounds were the kangany and the kanakapillai, who lead him to his quarry. He was the law, and there was no one to dispute it. He moved around in arrogance, in the knowledge of this fact.

38

'What are you doing here? Who asked you to come?' Hearing Thailammai's voice, Valli came out to investigate.

'Who are you to question me? You have become that bold, have you?' spat out Sengamalai who had returned home.

Valli was shocked by Thailammai's words.

'Why my child, why do you talk like that?' asked Valli.

'How should I talk? He not only drinks, but has brought shame upon us by taking to begging.'

'Ha, ha...,' laughed Sengamalai, mirthlessly. 'Oh, she is a great doraisani. She feels shame because her father begs!' he taunted her.

'Thailammai go inside! What's your problem? Are you the one feeding him?' asked Valli, angrily. She then invited him, 'Come, have some food. I have just cooked some hot rice.'

'Food, for me?' Sengamalai wept in anguish.

Valli's only felt pity for him. 'Why are crying? It is our fate! Come inside. I had gone to Kathirgamam. Thailai, bring some thiruneer, child!'

The word Kathirgamam wrought an immediate change in him. He stopped crying.

'Kathirgamam! Kathirgamam!' he repeated the words and started laughing aloud. 'Kathirgamam! Murugan! That god

Murugan, is he there for you and me? You are crazy! Crazy! God exists only for the rich, to deliver them from their sins. Why should people like you and me, who have done no harm to anyone pray to god? You crazy woman!' said Sengamalai bitterly.

Thailammai brought the thiruneer, and Valli applied it on his forehead. She felt his forehead burning with fever.

'What's wrong with you?' she asked.

'There is nothing wrong with me! Just a bad cough and fever. That will not get me down,' he sat down by the doorway, tired.

'Do you want a mat?'

'A mat? I have not seen one for a long time! Now that my final days are here, why do I need one?'

'Here, drink something hot,' said Thailammai, giving him some tea.

He got up with an effort, had tea and lay down again.

More than a week went by and the fever persisted. They took him to the hospital, but Sengamalai died within a week.

'Muruga! My life too has ended,' sobbed Valli. The moon spread its weak rays reflecting the state of Valli's mind. Bereft of hope, she sat in a corner, a broken woman.

Even though Sengamalai had been of no help to her in her daily struggles, somewhere she took heart from the feeling that he was alive. Now, even that solace had been snatched away from her.

39

That year the world witnessed the beginning of the second world war. This event brought about a few more changes to the plantation.

A new temple was built on the estate and a festival was to be held in the month of Chithirai.

'All you workers have to contribute towards the Mariamman poosai!' ordered the kangany.

Many workers came over from the neighbouring plantations to attend the Mariamman festival. Valli's daughter Meenakshi also came with her family. The air resounded with joy and excitement.

Valli remembered her childhood in India, where she witnessed similar festivals. They would scramble to get the kanji that was dished out by the devotees. She looked back fondly on those days.

Everyone waited for their wages at the office. It was Saturday. The Mariamman poosai was on Tuesday.

The kangany, sinna dorai, kanakapillai and the rest of the office staff were all seen in full strength.

The workers were standing outside, devising ways of giving the slip to their debtors. Although the government had asked the estate owners to wipe off the old debts, new debt had eventually cropped up. They owed money to the grocery store, the textile shops and to the Pathans who loaned them money at impossible interest rates. They were all waiting to collect their dues.

Times had changed, and now you could find small vendors gathered there, selling sweetmeats, colourful bangles, dolls for children, and saris in all hues that soon ran colour. The workers were torn between these alluring vendors and their hawk-eyed debtors.

'Dei, Muruga, come here,' the kangany beckoned Murugan.

'You must supervise the food arrangements for Tuesday. I have arranged for a Poosari, and musicians from Kandy. I have also asked them to bring four large garlands. The dorais will also be there.'

'Alright, ayya,' Murugan said.

'I am getting old, I want to finish all this work and go away.'

'Where will you go, ayya?' Murugan asked surprised. He could not imagine the kangany living anywhere other than on the plantation.

'Go back home, of course, now that my son is here. My younger son is studying in Colombo, and he wishes to go to England to study further. I don't know what I should do,' said the kangany with a sigh.

☙

It was finally Tuesday and it had been declared a holiday in honour of the festival. There was a lot of bustle and excitement by the river. Beautiful decorations adorned the temple. That small temple restored hope in the hearts of the workers.

'Meenakshi, your husband has come, come here,' Anjalai called to her sister.

'Ask him to wait, I am coming.'

'Kaveri's son was standing over here, where is he? Ask Kaveri to come soon. Tell her we have to go before the dorai and the rest arrive. It will take time to reach the lower division,' said Valli, as she combed Thailammai's hair and braided it. Conscious of modern ways, Thailammai did not bunch up her hair in the old-fashioned way.

Meenakshi's husband told Valli, 'Athai, I saw Lakshmanan last week at the fair. He said he is working in a tea shop.'

'As long as he's alright, it is ok. He is not allowed to enter the estate, you see,' said Valli to her son-in-law.

'Has my brother Sivasami come?'

'Yes, he has gone to the temple with Murugan. He wanted you to meet him there,' said Valli.

All of them proceeded to the temple.

Anjalai's forehead was adorned with thiruneer. The absence of the auspicious vermillion mark on her forehead affected Valli.

Thailammai looked attractive in her new clothes. Even the cheap sari she wore emphasised her beauty. Very soon she too will be married and gone, thought Valli.

'Is Kumaran working?' asked Meenakshi, about her brother.

'Yes, they have just given him a job weeding the grass. They have made Murugan a kanakapillai to supervise the weeding,' replied Valli.

Just then they heard the temple bells ringing and they hastened to the festival.

The kangany and the kanakapillai were standing at the entrance to the temple, dressed up in zari vettis and shawls. There was a small table with big brass plates. One was piled with garlands and the other with bananas, sugarcandy, kungumam, sandalwood paste, coconuts, etc. There were two chairs by the table. It was for the two dorais who were expected to attend the festival. Huge gas lights spread a bright light around the place. Coconut fronds and mango leaves were used as festoons. The fragrance of sandalwood, incense and camphor wafted in the air.

The smell of pongal and sundal being cooked made their mouths water. The workers momentarily forgot their careworn lives and participated in the festival with gusto.

The priest began the poosai to the sound of pipes and drums. The workers who had never seen such elaborate celebrations, were caught up by the excitement of the moment.

The dorais came on time to grace the occasion with their presence. The kangany welcomed them with garlands (much bigger than the one adorning the deity!), kunkumam and sandalwood paste.

Everyone appreciated the arrival of the two dorais. This gesture made them believe that the dorais wanted to be part of their joys and sorrows.

Valli was seated among the crowd, along with Anjalai and Meenakshi, watching their children play. Deivanai too joined them.

'Where is Thailammai?' asked Meenakshi.

'She is down with the other girls,' said Deivanai.

'Come sit down. We are thinking of Meenakshi's brother-in-law as a groom for Thailammai. What do you think?' asked Valli.

'If Thailammai likes him, we should go ahead with it,' answered Deivanai.

'Thalai says she does not wish to get married now.'

'People are already gossiping about her on the estate. It is better that Thailammai gets married soon,' said Anjalai.

'You can't stop gossip,' said Valli.

'They are gossiping about her and a married man. That Kandasamy is a terrible fellow. He is running around with young girls when he's got a beautiful wife at home,' said Deivanai.

'He is the kangany's son-in-law. He can do anything he wants. They are going to appoint him as the kangany for the new division. Our Rasa Estate is really going from bad to worse,' said Valli.

'The periya kangany is going back to India next month. The times are changing.'

Thailammai joined them bringing with her some of their relatives. They sat around and chatted awhile.

The other girls called out to Thailammai, 'Come join us! Why are you seated in a corner, alone.' They dragged her along and she joined them in dancing the kummi and kolattam.

The celebration went on all night.

'All of you, come join the feast,' called out the kangany and kanakapillai.

The festival soon came to an end.

Valli saw the periya dorai walking towards her and she got up respectfully.

'Valli, how are you?' he asked her in his usual manner with a smile on his face.

'I am doing alright, dorai,' said Valli, adjusting her sari.

'Where are your children?' he asked.

'They are all here.'

'Why do you still work? Why don't you ask your son to take care of you?' he said.

'Why should I dorai? As long as I am able to work, no one need feed me. As long as god gives me strength I can feed four more people. When you are there as our god, we have nothing to fear.'

'You are a tough one, Valli!' said the dorai, laughing.

'Yes dorai! Who can work like our Valli these days? That is why she is so haughty!' agreed the kangany.

'What sami! You have also joined with him,' Valli protested meekly, secretly pleased to have heard those words.

'Go now, go and eat!' the dorai said, as he walked away.

40

'Why is Thailai refusing to marry Meenakshi's brother-in-law?' asked Valli worriedly.

'How will she agree to the proposal when she is running around with that Kandasmay. She won't listen to anyone,' said Anjalai.

'It is all my fate! Alright… don't be annoyed now, but I hear Arunachalam visits you often, and he wants to marry you. Is it true?' Valli asked, a little unsure about Anjalai's reaction.

'Yes, so what? Marriage will not work for me. I can't think of another one.'

'How long can you live like this! At your young age…'

'What do you know mother? Today he will marry me because I am goodlooking, tomorrow when I have his child he will want to get rid of us. I know about these men, please don't interfere,' said Anjalai.

Valli was pained by her daughter's words 'It's your fate, what can I do? I can only advise you!'

'Alright, but ask Thailai to be cautious.'

'You think she listens to me? Would she then run around shamelessly like she does. If only there was someone to question her! Murugan is of no use, the moment he opens his mouth she pounces on him,' said Valli.

'As long as we are not disgraced, it is alright,' said Anjalai.

'You know Mari says he has had enough of school and is loafing around the town. Now that people can come and go as they please, a lot of people from the village have started coming to our estate to pick tea during the picking season.'

'What can we do about that? They have now brought a new law forbidding workers to be brought in from India. Because of this law, they now have Sinhala workers on all the rubber plantations. Arunachalam told me about it,' said Anjalai.

'During my days, we had to walk for ten days just to get to the overcrowded boat. These days they get into a train and they reach in three days without any pain or hassle,' said Valli.

'That's true, Arunachalam had gone to India last month for his mother's funeral and returned in two weeks. It would not have been possible earlier.'

'First of all they would not let people step out of the estate. Even now, at Kanakavalli Estate, they don't let anyone come or go, even for a wedding or a funeral. Deivanai's uncle is the kanakapillai there, he told us about it. I too would like to visit my village, but what can I do there? I would like to see my relatives again, but who would know me? You should taste the kanji made in our village—it used to smell so good and taste wonderful. Everything here is bland. But god has given prosperity to this country. I have not seen or heard of a single person die of starvation and it's been over fifty years since I came here.'

'I don't know much about our village, excepting for what I have heard from you.The sky is getting dark, it's threatening to rain. Get the clothes from the line before it starts raining. And did you hear, in the lower field there is a kind of disease eating the tea leaves?'

'Yes, they have brought pesticides from England to cure it,' said Valli.

The rain started falling steadily and soon poured in torrents. The kangany was looking for shelter from the rain. Valli invited him in and offered him a place to sit.

'Anjalai, make some hot tea for ayya,' said Valli.

'Don't bother, I don't want anything. As soon as the rain eases a little, I'll be on my way,' he said.

'It's no trouble ayya, can I get you some betel leaves?'

'No, don't bother. Do you know I am thinking of going back to India next month? I am tired of these mountains and the damp and the cold. I cannot work here any more. I am growing old, you see.'

'What is this ayya! Who will take care of this place if you go away?' asked Valli.

'What to do? My first wife insists that I come and settle the lands to my children before I die. I have no peace even in this old age. My younger son has gone to England. I do not know what to do till he returns.'

'Who will look after you work, ayya?'

'My eldest son will take over. But he is also finding it difficult, you know how these young people are. They cannot work like us. I have asked my son-in-law to take care of two divisions. The plantation is growing big every day.'

'My brother has also gone back to India for good. I wonder how he is,' mused Valli.

'I will look him up when I go to our village. You too have a few years of work left in you. What are you going to do after that? Look after your grandchildren and ask Murugan to take care of you.'

'What else can I do? I will work as long as I can manage and then take refuge in a place where I would get some food and die when the time comes,' said Valli. She had no plans for her future.

'Well, the rain has stopped, I will leave now.' The Kangany opened his umbrella and slowly walked away.

41

'I have been telling you that girl is running wild. Now she has run away with that Kandasamy fellow and they have gotten married in a temple. She's now his second wife. His first wife is a devil,' said Deivanai bitterly, as she served food for her husband Murugan.

'Give me some more curry. We can talk later. There is nothing that can be done, now that he has married her,' said Murugan.

'That's not all. The kangany is furious. He threatened to beat up Thailammai.'

'Those days have long gone! Do you think he can do something like that now and get away with it?'

'He may ask her to leave the estate.'

'Let him try! If that fellow leaves with Thailai it will only be a grave loss for his daughter…' said Murugan quite enjoying himself.

'You are always like this, never taking anything seriously… Go and comfort your mother. At her age, poor thing, she has to put up with all this.'

'Alright, serve some more rice. Mari is loafing around the countryside without listening to any one. This is all because of you. You are the one who spoils him by giving him money without my knowledge.'

'I am not the one giving him money, he gets it from his paati.'

'My mother does not have much to give him!'

'Not only your mother, he also gets money from my mother!'

'Somehow you've all managed to ruin him. When he comes home, send him to his grandfather. He said he has some job for him.'

'Alright, you go to your mother now.'

'That is where I am headed,' he said, and washed his hands and set out to meet Valli.

'If Arumugam comes here, tell him I will see him in the town next week.'

'He is a terrible fellow. Why are you friendly with him?'

'Don't worry, I just want to send a message through him.'

'Just be careful,' said Deivanai, still annoyed with him. Deivanai had five children, the eldest being Marimuthu. Marimuthu had been sent to an English-medium school in the town, with his grandfather's help. He had studied up to the eighth standard and dropped out from school, refusing to study any further. He also refused to work on the estate. His education made him assume that it was degrading to work on the estate.

'Dei Mari, what are you doing here?' asked Murugan, seeing his son hanging about with a few others at Valli's layyam.

Valli was seated in her room chewing betel leaves. Kumaran too had returned from work.

'Anna, Kandasamy has run away with our Thailai,' Kumaran told Murugan.

'Let him be, as long as he takes care of her we shouldn't worry. I just hope he doesn't kick her out into the streets after sometime.'

'The kangany is furious,' said Valli.

'As if he did not know what was going on for over three years? He is angry because his son-in-law has married her. Otherwise he would still pretend nothing was amiss. It's his wife who is very angry. We should be happy that Kandasamy has taken Thailai as his wife, that's something.'

'Well, the problem has been blown out of proportion by all these other women who have been discarded by him. Not a dog is interested in them now. They are now looking to avenge themselves on us,' said Valli, as she chewed her betel.

Murugan shared his mother's pain. 'What can we do Amma? We should be happy that he has married her. Let me talk to them, with time things will be alright. Look at me, I have been accepted now. Do you remember how displeased they were with my marriage?'

'They would never have been able to find a finer boy than you. How can they complain? But your sister is a girl, how will she deal with this all her life?' Valli worried about her daughter.

'Everything will work out, don't worry,' said Murugan.

'If that Kandasamy acts smart, he'll have to answer my knife,' said Kumaran.

'You better behave yourself. I have enough troubles and don't want you to add to them,' said Valli.

'If he harms Thailai in any way he will face the consequences. He better be good to her, otherwise I'll just chop his limbs with this pruning knife,' said Kumaran angrily.

There was a time when they would not have dared to express such sentiments. Kumaran's words shocked Valli. How the times have changed. Her tear filled eyes widened with incredulity. Was it her son who was talking like this? Can a labourer on the plantation talk so brazenly and get away with it? If he had spoken like this in those days, the punishment would have been severe. She remembered how her father Velan was once whipped mercilessly for having dared to question the kangangy.

Understanding his grandmother's fears, Mari said, 'Times have changed, paati. During these war times they give us weevil- and worm-filled rice in the ration shops, and there is a shortage even for clothes. Isn't this reason enough for a revolution?' asked Mari, amused by Valli's reaction.

'I don't understand any of this. At one time there was famine. But now there is plenty of everything and they still give us this worm-infested rice ...'

'Paati, do you want to see a picture in the bioscope?' asked Mari.

'Yes, in my old age that is all I need! But what is this bioscope?'

'Let me take you. You can see a drama without real people enacting it. It's all been filmed and you can watch it.'

'This is for young people like you. I don't need to watch it.'

'Well we are going to the town and will be back later,' said Mari, leaving with his friends. Kumaran too went along with them.

'You are the one who spoils him. He is loafing around, does not go to school and does not want to work. I hear he now smokes,' said Murugan.

'Let him be. You have been working from your younger days, what have you to show for it? Let him have his fun,' said Valli, defending her grandson.

'I hear he is going around with the Sinhala boys in the village, and has learnt to drink,' said Murugan.

'Don't worry, he'll settled down.'

'It is my fate!'

'At his age that is how they are. He will be alright once he begins to work.'

'Well, he's refusing to do that.'

'He will work, give him time. I will have a talk with him.'

42

Valli felt an urge to visit her youngest daughter. Soon after weighing her tea leaves she walked towards her daughter's layyam.

These days she was relieved that her grandson Mari too had started working. She soon reached Thailai's layyam.

'Whore! Paraya whore, you have come to destroy my family!' raged a woman.

'Let me go or I'll scream! Am I a bitch or are you?' Thailammai's voice reached Valli.

Shocked, she stood rooted to the spot. She could hear both their voices loud and clear.

'You are the bitch! You must have charmed him with some black magic. I will kill you now before I do anything else!'

'Do it if you dare! Are you going to leave or not?'

Valli heard a loud thud.

'You witch! You wicked devil! May you be afflicted by cholera! May you come down with chicken pox!'

She heard the loud curses. Unable to tolerate it any longer Valli rushed to the layyam.

Thailammai and Kandaswamy's first wife, Angammal, were locked in a fight.

'You think you can get rid of me? You don't know me. You better stay away from my husband or else I will see to it that you are driven out of this estate!'

'Is this your father's estate? Try and chase me out, let's see,' Thailai said with a sneer.

Workers on their way back home stood there watching the fun.

'If you can keep your husband to yourself, do that. Why do you have to quarrel with her!' said Valli, springing to her daughter's defense.

By then a crowd had gathered in front of the layyam. Not wishing to speak anymore, Valli returned to her home. This incident left her disturbed and shaken.

By the time she reached her layyam it was dark. One or two tin lamps could be seen flickering in the rooms.

Mari and Kumaran were seated outside, talking intently.

'You are a fool! All of you are fools!' said Mari in a frustrated voice.

'Why do you say that?' asked Kumaran.

'Don't you know, why? You should go out and talk with others to know what is going on in the country. Only then will you know the truth. They don't want us to be aware of the changes taking place in the country, that's why they shut us all up here, like chickens in a coop!'

'But we do go to the town these days.'

'Yes, but that is only to sell vegetables, chicken and the like. The government has opened a labour office in the town and the plantation owners cannot do as they please, like they used to.'

'What kind of talk is this? This will only land us in trouble. My brother Lakshmanan talked about the union and was driven out of the estate.'

'Times have changed. We are going to ask for a raise in the wages! This whole place will stink without us,' said Mari.

'Go on, you are just talking big,' said Kumaran.

'What is all this talk, as if you are going to change the world?' asked Valli, as she joined them.

'What do you know about it paati?' asked Mari.

Valli laughed, amused by her grandson's smart talk. Even though she was proud of him, she also feared his ways.

'You better take care of yourself. You don't have to teach me anything, my life is over,' said Valli.

'All our lives will come to an end with time. It's not going to happen just to you, paati.'

'Just be careful. Don't throw sand on your own head like your chithappa. I hope god gives you some good sense.'

'Now tell me, will you come with us this year to the Kandy Perahera festival? Now that the war is over, they are going to have the festival again this year.' Mari cleverly changed the subject of discussion.

'Let us see,' Valli replied.

Time rolled by, the second world war came to an end, but famine took hold of the land. There was shortage of food and clothing—even blankets to protect them from the cold were not available. The workers were forced to make do with sack-cloth, but the material provided inadequate protection. They shivered through the cold nights and wet days.

That year, as Mari said, the Kandy Perahera was celebrated with great fervour and enthusiasm. Valli went with Murugan and his family to watch it.

Elephants decorated with elaborate gold-embroidered satins were paraded with pride. All night, the dancers entertained the crowds and the place resounded with drumbeats and fireworks. This festival has been celebrated from the ancient times and people look forward to it even today.

Valli had heard about the legend of Sanghamitra and Mahindra, King Ashoka's children, who visited Sri Lanka to spread Buddhism. With them they had brought a sapling of the famous Bodhi tree, under which Buddha attained enlightenment, and the Buddha's tooth as a relic. This tooth was placed in a casket and a temple was built in its honour.

Valli watched the Kandy festivities with stupefied amazement. She remembered the Natarasankottai annual festival she was taken to as a child by her parents. Valli felt herself becoming a child again, as she took in all the wonders around her.

43

With changing times, Valli's hopes and expectations had been pushed around so much that she had no clue as to who she was or what she wanted from life. She had witnessed the lives of three generations of her family since she came to the estate. But she still had not figured out where they were headed.

In the evenings, she sat by her doorway and watched the distant hills, fields, tumbling water cascades and the few buildings that had cropped up here and there. Everything seemed alien to her. Like the fog that visited them regularly, some strange feeling obscured her thoughts, pressing upon her daily life.

She went inside for a drink of water. She found that there was no water in the pot. 'The pot is empty. I seem to have forgotten even to fetch water. These days I am becoming very forgetful, nothing seems right,' she said to herself, as she took the pot to fetch water.

She saw that the rose and jasmine bushes, planted by Thailammai, were fragrant with blossoms. 'Since that child left, they have not been watered properly' she thought to herself.

Since she had come home early from work that day, she had plenty of time before dark. She saw the kangany on the way and asked him, 'Ayya, are you leaving for India tomorrow?'

'Yes, it is no use staying here any longer. My son is arriving from England tomorrow. I will meet him in Colombo and then leave for India. His mother too is looking forward to seeing him,' said the kangany, with pride.

'I pray that everything works out well, ayya.'

'Even the dorai wants to leave. He is waiting for orders from England.'

'Who, our periya dorai? If he too goes away, then what will happen to us?' she exclaimed.

'A new dorai will take charge. After working all these years for this dorai, it will not be easy for me to work for a new man. I wish to leave before that happens,' The kangany shared his apprehensions with Valli.

'I wonder what is going to happen to us!'

'Now that they have established a labour department, the dorais can't harass you any more,' said the kangany.

'Still, it was so much better in those days,' said Valli, emphatically.

The kangany was briefly reminded of the once attractive Valli of those times.

'Your working days are also coming to a close,' he said with a sigh and bade her goodbye. Valli watched him walk away, still straight backed and brisk. Age did not seem to have slowed him down.

While she was returning home, Valli heard the sound of laughter behind the bushes. The faint rumble of the machines in the factory could still be heard, much like a man struggling to breathe. She could see the workers moving around in the factory. But what caught her attention was the indistinct voices and laughter behind the bushes.

She strained her eyes to identify the source of laughter. But the dense bushes and growing darkness did not aid her cause. The tinkling laughter of a woman floated in the wind, pleasantly mingling with the distant gurgling of the river.

Valli was shaken when she realised who the lovers behind the bushes were—they were none other than her grandson, Mari, and the Sinhala girl, Menika. She was the daughter of Banda, who came to work on the estate during the tea-picking season. Valli felt her water pot shake and spill. She heard her grandson, whom she still thought was a boy say, 'I wish to marry you soon, alright?'

'I wonder what my mother will say?'

'Let her protest, I'll just carry you away.'

There was that laughed again.

Menika was indeed a beauty! Her beautifully moulded figure, her lush breasts which peeked over her low cut blouse, her dark eyes, were all delightful. Silver bangles tinkled in her hands. Her dimpled smile added to her allure.

Valli's head reeled. Menika was a Sinhala girl. How did this happen? Of course, she was quite goodlooking and almost all the young men had an eye on her.

It was dark by the time Valli reached her layyam.

Her mind was in turmoil, caused by the realisation that her grandson was now a grown man.

'Atha, where have you been?' Valli heard the concerned voice of her son Murugan.

'I went to the river to fetch water.'

'I asked you not to do that? Where is Kumaran?'

'He has not returned from work.'

'What would happen if you slipped down those slopes!'

Murugan gazed at his mother. He took in her sunken cheeks, her ungroomed hair that badly needed oil and comb, and saw that she had aged. But years of toiling had not bent her back. He suddenly remembered what his son Mari had said the other day.

'Are we workers not human beings? Why should we be treated like cattle and sheep? Have you seen any of these tea bushes wilt and droop? See how carefully they tend and care for those plants, hoeing the ground, fertilising and pruning them regularly. Why isn't the same concern shown for our welfare? Don't we have wishes and desires? Are we meant to end our lives wearing these rags, living amongst rubbish, driven to drinking? Look at this room, is it enough to run a family? Even their chicken coops are bigger, their cattle sheds more spacious…'

Murugan was impressed by his son's argument, and the fervour he had exhibited.

Valli's summons to come in and have some tea woke him from his reverie.

'I am worried about Mari, he is running wild and will not listen to anyone. He says he is going to marry a Sinhala girl. He also seems to be creating trouble on the estate. This has even reached the dorai's ears. He has already warned him. You must also speak to him about this.'

'Youngsters these days are like that! Don't worry.' Even as she comforted her son, a nameless fear took possession of Valli.

But Murugan found it difficult to get over his apprehension.

'We are the people who should change. As Mari said, we have been the fools, putting up with this for all these years. Our days are over, let him be, don't try to change him,' advised Valli.

'I have said what I had to say. Deivanai is crying her eyes out.'

'Ask her to go the temple, light a lamp and make a vow. Everything will be alright.' Valli herself did not know how much faith she had in what she said.

ℭ

One fine day, Mari appeared at his parent's home, with his newly wed wife Menika. Though Murugan and Deivanai knew about their affair, they had not anticipated the marriage.

Seeing her husband Murugan standing at the doorway, Deivanai quietly went in, not willing to intrude.

Looking at the newly wed couple, Murugan was reminded of the time he had eloped with Deivanai. This thought vanquished his rising anger and he understood Mari's plight. He felt sympathy for Mari.

Menika looked lovely as she stood there, looking at the ground, her toes tracing patterns on the earth. Even the usually brash Mari looked a little disconcerted and unsure of himself.

An uneasy silence kept them frozen.

Murugan's youngest son came running over and asked his brother 'Who is this, anna?'

This broke the silence.

'Go inside and have some tea,' said Murugan to the couple.

Deivanai was amazed by Murugan's reaction. Normally, he was a loving person, but when angered he could get quite violent. She was gladdened by his easy acceptance and rushed to invite her son and his wife.

'Come, come in Menika.' Mari led his wife inside.

Murugan was taken up by Menika's quiet manner, the open affection on her face, and the beauty that shone through her eyes.

'Amma, Menika does not know much Tamil. You must teach her,' said Mari, introducing his wife to his parents.

'She will learn soon,' said Deivanai. 'What about her parents? Where are they?'

'It was with their permission that I married her. They have a little farm in the village. They grow some corn and rice.'

'I wonder what your grandfather is going to say to this,' said Deivanai, as the thought struck her.

'Don't worry, I will take care of that. He knows our Menika very well,' said Murugan confidently.

'Well, it is between the two of you. He brought you up dearly, because he had no sons. He believed one day you will take up his job, instead you seem to be running around like this.'

'What? I can never be a kanakapillai. I can't run behind all the young girls on the estate. Only he can do that,' joked Mari, smiling at Menika, who returned the smile.

Deivanai witnessed this exchange quietly.

'Menika will stay here, she will not be returning to the village.'

Deivanai was discomfited by the thought of more people in that small room and the lack of privacy for the newly wed couple. As if he had read her mind, Mari said, 'I will ask thatha for a room of my own.'

'There are so many who have been waiting for years for a room. The estate is filled with such people. How can he give you one now?' asked Deivanai.

'Thatha will give me one, alright. I will see to that,' said Mari confidently.

44

For creating disturbance and organising the workers against the management, Mari was handed over to the police by the dorai.

'I cannot understand what's going on,' said Valli to Murugan.

'It seems they had planned to set fire to the store. They have arrested ten men in this regard,'

'Why?'

'They have started something called the labour union. They are asking for human rights and freedom from bondage. Foolish fellow, instead of being the kanakapillai, he has earned trouble,' Murugan said in frustration.

'What can we do now? Only the lord Muniyan can save him.'

'A new dorai has arrived to take charge. Our old dorai is leaving tomorrow for England.'

'Is he going tomorrow?' asked Valli, feeling lost.

'Yes, he was supposed to leave next week, but he received a telegram saying his wife was ill, so he is leaving tomorrow.'

'You better talk to your father-in-law and see if something can be done. It is bad times for us now.'

'What can he do? The dorai has insisted that Mari leave the estate. He has asked the office to give him his dismissal papers.'

'So soon?'

'Yes, the moment the dorai heard that Mari was making trouble, he asked the office to issue the dismissal. He has ordered him out of the estate.'

'What will they do to him at the police station?' asked Valli, fearing his safety.

'Who knows?'

Days passed, and the workers anxiously waited the outcome of this latest event.

Maclean left the estate and the new dorai, Andrews, took charge. He was devoid of sympathy, compassion and fairplay. His only aim was to make profit for his bosses in England and earn their appreciation. He was a forbidding figure, with a stern and stony face.

'What a world of difference between the old dorai and the new one,' thought Valli to herself.

The day he was leaving for England, Maclean was garlanded and given an elaborate send off. Valli cried inconsolably and fell at his feet, as she thanked him for everything.

Valli felt deep affection for him. He had been like a parent to the workers.

They felt like orphaned children at his departure. Valli had felt a similar sense of loss when she had heard of her father Velan's death.

ɞ

'They are going to hold an inquiry at the labour office,' said Murugan.

'Why? Is this regarding our Mari?'

'Yes, and the new dorai has asked Menika to leave the estate.'

'Why?'

'He has issued his orders—they cannot stay on the estate. But she has refused to leave. Mari has asked her not to leave till the inquiry is over at the labour office.'

'What will they do if she refuses to go?' asked Valli.

'What else? They will throw her out! Let us see what happens...'

The new dorai did not listen to anyone. He could not be moved. The police inquiry was over and Mari was sentenced to three months imprisonment. Mari's wife was forcibly evicted from the estate. She was asked never to return or enter the estate.

'Get out! Don't ever step foot on the estate again! Understand?' said the dorai, as he had her removed from the estate.

The other workers did not interfere and life went on as usual on the estate.

'Atha,' Kumaran called out to his mother.

'What is it son? You know these days my eyesight is failing, I am not able to see properly!'

'Atha, give me some tea. I am going to the town, Mari is being released from prison today!'

'I too would like to come,' said Valli eagerly.

'Let me go see him first. It seems they have planned a big welcome for him. I am just going to find out about it.'

Valli was intrigued by the piece of information.

'What is the welcome for?'

'He is the first person in these parts who had dared to fight against the injustice perpetrated on us workers. So people have decided to make him the leader of the union.'

'All this is new to me,' said Valli, and suddenly she felt her legs give way and she collapsed on the floor.

'Atha, atha...' Kumaran called out to her and tried to revive her.

He sprinkled some water on her face, and called out to his neighbours for help.

Valli soon gained consciousness and made an attempt to sit up.

'What is it, atha? Are you alright? Anything wrong with your health?' asked Kumaran with concern.

'It's nothing, just felt a little faint. After all I am old, you know.'

Yes, Valli had indeed grown old!

Kumaran was reminded of the kangany advising the new dorai to lay off the old women and employ younger women.

As expected, one day, the new kangany told Valli, 'Valli, you cannot work any more, why don't you retire and take your pension?'

'But ayya, please let me work a little longer,' she protested.

'We have to give work to the young ones. Next month I will arrange for your pension.'

'What can I do if you pension me off so soon? How much will I get?' asked Valli in a worried tone.

'I will talk to the office and ask them to give you a good deal. I will also speak about you to the dorai. You have been here for so long. I will ask them to give you five rupees and half a measure of rice. You don't really have to worry, you have your sons,' said the kangany.

'But ayya, five rupees? That will not feed me for the rest of my life.'

'Nothing more can be done. At least you are getting this, the others won't get so much. Do you understand?'

Valli was dumbfounded. Tears blinded her eyes. She tried to suppress the tears and the rage that threatened to overwhelm her.

'After having worked all my life, is this all I get ayya?'

'Yes, how many times do I have to tell you?' he replied in an irritated voice.

Valli walked away in rage. But before she could reach her layyam, she heard a loud commotion. Without paying much heed to it she kept walking, only to find the noise grow louder.

Bewildered, she stopped on her tracks and looked around. At a distance, she saw a long procession marching through the estate.

As the crowd neared her, the noise grew louder and louder.

'Long live the workers! Long live the workers! We want our rights! We want our rights!' Their cries were charged with emotion and it felt like it would split the sky.

Valli moved aside. The crowd was approaching her. They marched in endless rows, weaving their way through the estate.

Who is that leading the crowd? Yes, no doubt about it. It was Mari! Was her grandson the person leading this crowd? Valli stood transfixed.

Going past her, the crowd walked towards the dorai's bungalow.

'Long live the labourers! Long live the labourers!' they shouted in unison.

Yes, they should live long. There was a promise there in those words. Valli felt the excitement in the air.

Mari went past, without even noticing her. She felt that he was no longer merely her grandson. He had found a new path for himself.

But she did not really understand his way of life.

Suddenly there was a confusion among the workers. A cavalcade of motor vehicles rushed towards them.

A police contingent got down from the vehicles and tried to stop the crowd. But they refused to comply and kept marching bravely, 'Long live labourers! Long live labourers!' Their shouts became more strident and powerful.

Suddenly they heard gunshots ringing through the crowd. Valli was shocked and astounded. She hastened towards the sound, stumbling and staggering, her legs failing her.

'Mari, Mari!' she screamed out her grandson's name.

The crowd dispersed. Those who had fallen on the ground were carried and pushed into the vehicles.

'Mari, Mari,' screamed Valli, as she ran after the vehicle.

'Stay away from here, nothing has happened to me!' She heard her grandson Mari's strict injunction. Murugan stopped her from going further.

'Atha, don't go there!'

'Let me go! Who is that? It is Kumaran, isn't it? They are taking him away in that vehicle,' she sobbed inconsolably and tried to get to the vehicles. But the people around her would not let her go.

By then the motor vehicles had left, weaving their way out like deadly cobras.

'Aiyo, my son! Aiyo, is this the way my life should end...' Valli beat her chest and lamented aloud.

Murugan consoled her and led her to her layyam.

The next day they received the news that Kumaran had died in the hospital.

They brought the corpse to the estate.

'How many more have I to sacrifice before I die? You too have thrown dirt in my womb and have left me! You sinner!' sobbed Valli.

The tea bushes flourish, bursting with vitality, having fed on the corpses of these hapless workers. Valli reviled them, 'You heartless monsters!'

Those enjoying their daily cup of hot tea, how will they ever know the story behind this wonderful brew?

GLOSSARY

Aadi	Fourth month in the Tamil calendar, mid-July to mid-August
Ambalam	A large thatched resting shed for travellers
Angavastram	A piece of cloth (sometimes embroidered with gold and silver threads) worn on the shoulder by men
Anna/Annachi	Elder brother
Appa/Appu	Father
Atha	Mother
Athai	Aunt
Ayya	Sir/Father
Cheri	A ghettoized village within a village, where the Scheduled castes live
Chettiar	A caste Hindu community, usually involved with money-lending and trade
Chinnaiya	Uncle (Father's younger brother)
Chithappa	Father's younger brother
Chithirai	The first month of the Tamil calendar, mid-April to mid-May
Dorai	The white man who is usually the boss
Doraisani	The dorai's wife (usually a white woman)
Elandai (Ilanthai)	A thorny tree yielding edible red berries
Ey/Ele/Dei	Expression used to order people with authority and also disrespect
Kaman Kuthu	A type of folk play
Kambarisi	Millet
Kanakapillai	Accountant

Kangany	Supervisor
Kanji	Gruel
Kolattam	Folk dance performed with short sticks
Kummi	Folk dance performed by women
Kungumam	A bright red mark, normally worn on the forehead by women
Kuthuvilakku	Oil-lamp ritually lit in homes and temples
Layyam	A dwelling with several rooms (arranged in a line) for the plantation labourers; each room was usually occupied by a large family
Lungi	A lower garment used by men
Machan	Kinship term used by wives to address their husbands; also used to refer to one's brother-in-law
Mama	Uncle
Margazhi	Ninth month of the Tamil calendar, mid-December to mid-January
Masi	Eleventh month of the Tamil calendar, mid-February to mid-March
Mirasdar	A rich landlord commanding a high status in a village
Moodevi	Goddess of misfortune (Derogatory usage)
Murukku	A crispy snack made with rice and spices
Murungai	Moringa tree; tree which yields drumsticks
Oyilattam	A type of folk dance performed with colourful pieces of cloth
Paati	Grandmother
Paraya	An aboriginal agricultural community who were forced to do menial jobs and were considered untouchables

Pavadai	Long skirt
Periatha	Father's first wife
Periya	Elder/Big
Poosai	Religious festival; ritual
Pournami	Full moon (day)
Puvarasan	Portia tree
Sami	A respectful mode of address equivalent to 'Sir'
Saniyan	A curse word referring to the planet Saturn
Sembu	A vessel with a narrow neck, usually used to carry water, milk, etc.
Sinna	Younger/Small
Sollam (Cholam)	A variety of grain
Sunnambu	Lime paste
Thandai	Thick anklets
Thandora	A kind of drum beaten to announce death or proclaim some news
Thatha	Grandfather
Thavani	Also known as half-sari, it is an upper garment worn over a long skirt, by young girls
Thinnai	A small raised platform in the verandah of a house
Thiruneer	Holy ash
Vetti	White cloth worn as a lower garment by men